Burnt Roses

A Witherspoon Adventure

Mary Devlin Lynch
and
Debbie Devlin Zook

with
Beth Devlin-Keune

© 2010 Mary Devlin Lynch/Debbie Devlin Zook
Revised 2014
All rights reserved
Published by *Devlinsbooks*

ISBN No. 978-0-615-39118-2

To our children—Megan and Peter, Scott and Wendy—who are the inspiration for everything we do. They are supportive of our dreams just as we are of theirs. And to our grandchildren, Collin, Luke, and Zachary, who are our legacies.

Prologue

There is always a moment, a pivotal moment in life, when you can point a finger, and say, "See? That was it. That's when everything changed forever." Perhaps you were planning for it, praying for it, and then it's a joyous event. But sometimes it's thrust upon you without your consent. Sometimes it's like a tidal wave sweeping in, washing away everything you have and leaving you clinging to what's left of your life trying to figure out a way to survive.

Melissa Sullivan hadn't seen it coming any more than her father had known there would be a hay baler blocking the road when he drove his pickup around the turn.

Slow motion, that's how Melissa remembered it. Her mother screamed and turned her head to look for Melissa, who was riding in the bed of the truck. Had she screamed for Melissa to jump? Her father eyes met hers in the rearview mirror for a split second. Had he told her to jump or had she just read it in his eyes?

Melissa jumped over the side seconds before the two moving pieces of metal slammed into each other, before the gas and oil caught fire. She dropped and rolled into the scratchy cornstalks.

Her parents' last thoughts were only for her and she'd never told anyone. She held those moments close to her heart and she carried a copy of the yellowed newspaper clipping in her wallet dated July 23, 1996.

Popular Local Couple Killed in Accident
   by Charles Hayden, Editor
Rob and Emily Sullivan, 35 and 34, respectively, died instantly in a vehicular accident yesterday on Old Airport Road. Their pickup truck struck a hay baler owned by Frank Wheeler which was attempting to cross the road. Their daughter, Melissa, riding in the back of the truck, was miraculously thrown clear.

The article went on to detail the couple's involvement in the community, as members of the Baptist Church, the Grange, library fund-raising campaign, etc. It ended with a sharp rebuke to the DOT for failing to do something about those dangerous blind curves on Old Airport Road.

Once the grief and anger subsided, bitterness settled in. Melissa was snatched from the warmth of her parents' shabby but comfortable farm house and dumped on Mimi Witherspoon in that horrendous old house on Witherspoon Lane, a house that was not meant for children. At eleven, Melissa had planned her life: she would become a writer, marry a local man, have three children and live happily ever after in Sylvan Mills, the town her forefathers had founded. Period.

Enter the turning point—exit the happily ever after. She lived with Mimi and her Aunt Jane until she graduated high school, then they shipped her off to college in New York. Melissa, adrift with no anchor at eighteen, tried to move on with her career, find the right man, and make a home for herself. But nothing felt right; nothing filled the empty spaces. Even though she knew she should get over it and be happy with what she had, somebody owed her a life; the life she'd always wanted and should have had.

Melissa had promised herself she would never set foot in that town again until Mimi was dead. She would go back for the funeral, just to make sure. She often prayed that would be soon. But when her Aunt Jane called to tell her that Mimi was dying and begged her to come home, Melissa saw her chance to get some closure for what her therapist called "unresolved issues."

For the first time in eight years, Melissa was going home and this time she was going to get what was coming to her.

CHAPTER ONE

"Sleeping Beauty has landed in the cuckoo's nest, my friend, and I saved her just for you." Connie Torres-Garcia, the head nurse on the day shift, flashed Stephen her gleaming smile and slapped the metal chart into his hand. "She is so clean I cain't hardly stand it. Turns out County's got a 'lectrical problem. Took out a whole wing and they're crammed with treehuggers what chained themselves to those trees and got all splintered up out there in Westchester. It was in the papers. Don't you read? So we're gettin' some overflow and this one's a gift from me to you."

He glanced at the chart and then returned the smile. He leaned down and whispered, "You're my favorite person in this whole place."

"Humph. Like that's some hot competition." She gave him a gentle shove and he practically ran down the hall to see his new patient.

She was a gift, all right, he thought, staring at the ivory hand with neatly trimmed nails laying against the starched sheet; a gift and a startling reminder of what he had gotten used to: rotted teeth, dirty broken nails, arms that had no veins left that would hold a needle. Sad street people who wore hats to keep their heads on and the voices out, cons in training for Rikers, these were his usual patients. It had taken awhile, but now he joined in the staff pools, betting on how long each one would last outside before being picked up and delivered back to Riverview.

At first he had found it callous, but then he began to understand. It was the black humor of police stations or the morgue, he now realized, where jokes made at the most inappropriate times were the only shields against the horror of their daily work. Leaning forward, he studied the white streak in her light brown hair. It was just at her part line on the right side and was shorter than the other roughly cropped pieces. Aha, attacking the inherited family trait with a vengeance. He breathed in the fresh scent of her skin, then turned and stood looking out of the bars that covered the window. He hated those bars.

What was she doing here?

He suddenly had the sensation of being watched. He turned to face her even as the flush that always came too easily crept up his neck. He rubbed a hand across his scratchy chin. Her eyes were shut tightly but he had not imagined the flash of color, golden brown, no, maybe hazel. No matter, what did matter was that she had seen him, the first step into accepting him, trusting him. He stood silently by her side for another minute or two before crossing the room and closing the door behind him.

The chart was a simple one with more blanks than information:

Name: Unknown
Description: Caucasian female
Admitted by: Unknown male
Condition: Unconscious
Treatment: Gastric lavage—removed unknown
quantity of Xanax from stomach

Unknown. The odd sensation he was feeling must be an adrenaline rush. He unlocked the door to his office, stepped inside, and relocked it carefully, leaving the key in the lock. He had rebelled against that, too, when he was new here, until Connie had taken him aside.

"Look, Doc, I understand where you comin' from, but you must follow procedures. Doors are locked from the inside and the key left in the lock, got it?"

"No, I don't get it." He had shrugged. "So what if some poor bastard wants to bum a cigarette. This isn't a prison."

She sighed her Connie-the-martyr sigh and leaned into him, getting as close as she could to his face. "Listen, Dr. Do-Good, we don't make this shit up, ya know. It's not just your office. If you don't care if you walk in here and find everything gone, fine by me. But wait till you're in the john and see an eyeball lookin' at you through the keyhole, or get yourself stabbed with your own pen and see how that plays. You think this ain't no prison, you look again, child, 'cause at least half of these folks come straight from Rikers."

At the stricken look on his face, she added, "Uh-huh" with a nod and marched out the door, muttering to herself, "Lord, save me." She waited in the hallway until she heard the key turn.

He might not agree, but he got it. So he locked the doors, always made sure that patients preceded him down the stairs, followed all the other idiotic rules, and took the money.

He threw himself into the grubby metal chair and scribbled his name as fast as he could on the stack of paperwork on his desk so he could go have another look at his new patient.

There was a soft tap at the door. "It's Connie, doc. Open up."

He turned the key and she motored inside, all business. "Hey, good lookin'. Looks like Ms. Snow White's boyfriend grew a pair and called her family. Some old lady's been rippin' heads off upstairs and she is outta here. Thought I'd stop by and pick up the chart. The chief hisself called it down." She grabbed the chart holder and hustled back to the door before it struck her that he hadn't said a word. "Hey, ya know what they says 'bout things bein' too good to be true, right?" She turned, walked behind his desk, and laid a warm hand on his shoulder. "Ya okay, doc?"

He nodded around the lump blocking his throat and massaged his forehead with long fingers.

"What's her name?" He muttered.

She sighed. "Now you got no need to know that. I been told in no uncertain terms by the man what signs my paycheck that this girl was never here. Get it? Before this day is out, her fairy tale will continue at some private fa-cil-i-ty where she will recover from exhaustion or faintin' spells or somethin' prettier than an OD."

He didn't respond so she continued. "Are we clear? No chart, no patient, no name. I don't even know what we're talkin' 'bout." She took a breath.

"I get it. Thought you was gonna hit a home run here, didn't ya? I'm sorry, Stephen. You just keep the faith, baby. Mmmm, mmmm." She headed for the door then turned back towards him. "So I am tellin' you that as far as we concerned, *Melissa Sullivan* was never here." She winked and walked out.

Melissa. She was leaving and that was absolutely right. She should never have been here in the first place. But Stephen knew a wake-up call when he got one. He had turned into one of the bureaucratic hacks he despised, riding the system, playing "here we go 'round the mulberry bush" with the chronically mentally ill because it was a damned good living.

He closed his eyes and allowed himself to imagine working with this girl. Hell, she actually had a home and family to go back to, unlike 99% of his patients.

He couldn't help himself; he stood by the barred window and watched her leave.

In the glare of the afternoon sun, the dark splotches under her eyes were shadowed bruises and the short, chopped hair a halo. As the wheelchair was rolled up to the side of the dark town car and she was safely deposited in the back seat, he could have sworn she looked up to where he stood at one of twenty identical narrow windows covered by thin black bars, but that was ridiculous.

At five, he trudged down to the nurses' station, signed out, and then jogged to his Porsche, always parked in the back row away from the other cars. The security guard in the booth gave him a thumbs-up. Stephen was generous at

Christmas and remembered his kids' names, so the guard kept a close eye on the gleaming sports car. The soft leather bucket seat usually soothed Stephen's frustrations, but not today.

He sat there and stared at Riverview. Rumor had it the original design had been lovely, pristine white cubes with flowers, a central lawn, and leaded glass doors. Then some politicians in Albany decided the island location made it a perfect treatment center, i.e., dumping ground, for "special needs" patients. Barred windows and steel doors changed the effect. As the patients trampled the flowers, the lawn died and the buildings were soon trying to hide behind damp, mossy coats.

Rumor also had it that the talented young architect had burst into tears every time he passed it until concerned friends convinced him to move to L.A. Stephen knew exactly how he felt. His time at Riverview was over. He was already gone; he had left long ago but had never allowed himself to admit it until now because of a chance encounter with a young woman named Melissa Sullivan.

CHAPTER TWO

He wondered what had happened to her more than once, but he wasn't the type to track her down. So fate, yes, *serendipity*, had to step in and lend him a hand.

One rainy evening in Manhattan, the main window in Barnes and Noble was alight with spinning silver-jacketed books hung on transparent wires and more of the same stacked and spiraled in a dazzling display of "Who Am I?" It was impossible to pass the window without looking at them and Stephen joined the crowd. Pressing closer, he saw that the window also featured several smiling cardboard cutouts of the author's face plastered with a banner: BOOK SIGNING TODAY.

He was on his way to Broadway to see a show with his former college girlfriend, Tiffany. He looked at his watch and decided not to bother calling her to say he'd be late; she wouldn't be surprised. He was always late, give or take 20 minutes. It was simply a matter of always thinking he had more time than he did; time to squeeze in one more thing. Stephen's heart was pounding as he stepped into the wide aisle surrounded by bookshelves. The author was seated at a table near the back.

Someone came through the door behind him and ran into him; he had been standing in the middle of the aisle with his mouth hanging open while he stared. He moved sideways into the stacks and watched her for a few more minutes. *It really was her.* His brain seemed to be stuck repeating it. *What should he do?* Should he buy a book and take it over to her? There were at least a dozen people in line. He looked at his watch again.

Tiffany would have a hissy fit if the last call lights started flickering at the theater. She had made a big deal out of offering him her extra ticket to this sold-out show. With a mental sigh, Stephen hustled toward the door of the bookstore.

A clerk wearing a green vest intercepted him and thrust a copy of the book into his hand. "Courtesy of the author," he smirked. Stephen took it and ran out the door. It wasn't until after the show, in the privacy of his own apartment, that he opened the cover. "Call me," it said, with a number below.

It took him several days to work up the nerve to make the call. He had practiced the conversation many times before dialing the number; he wasn't an impulsive man.

"Melissa Sullivan." A crisp voice answered.

"Hi, this is, uh, Stephen Callahan. From the, uh, bookstore ..."

Her laughter tinkled through the line. "And from Riverview, right? After a couple of days, I figured maybe I'd been mistaken and scared the hell out of some innocent bystander."

He cleared his throat. "I, uh, used to be at Riverview."

The name caused them both to go quiet for a few seconds, and then she graciously moved on, "Stephen, huh?"

"Yes, Stephen spelled with a 'p-h.'"

"Well, Stephen with a 'p-h,' now that we're on a first name basis, can I buy you dinner?"

He cleared his throat, and heard Tiffany's voice in his head say, *Do not say that the gentleman always buys, you idiot. Be cool.* "Sure. Yes. I'd like that."

"Good. Would you mind coming here? It's been a long week and I have another early day tomorrow. I'm at The Pierre."

He was struggling to listen as fast as she talked. "No problem. What time?"

There was a moment of silence and he knew she was checking her watch. "How about seven? That gives you roughly three hours to think up a way to get out of it."

He didn't want her to think him inexperienced with women. He wasn't really, just simply sometimes; well, awkward at first dates. Once he and Tiffany had figured out they weren't meant to be life partners, she had tried to help him along the path to the right woman. Her number one rule was - *Always meet them for a drink first. That way you (or they) can make an excuse and run.* He said firmly, "Seven's great. I'll meet you at the bar."

It was as if he could feel her smiling on the other end of the line. "Perfect. Do you think we'll recognize each other or should I wear a red carnation?"

"We'll recognize each other."

Her tone changed in response to the quiet conviction in his voice. "Of course we will."

Promptly on the hour and on time for maybe the first time in his life, Stephen folded his tall body onto a bar stool and wished he'd worn a lighter jacket.

Within minutes, she slid onto the stool next to him. "So here we are."

"Yes, here we are. You, uh, look wonderful."

Her easy laugh made him smile. "Compared to the first time you saw me, anyway."

Thankfully, their table was ready by the time their drinks came. He had a lot of questions but wasn't absolutely sure he wanted to know the answers.

"I don't suppose you've read my book yet?" She opened.

He shifted in his seat and cleared his throat. "I, uh ..." How could he say that it had somehow seemed like an invasion of her privacy? Or maybe that he didn't really want to know? Or that he was an incredibly slow reader, with piles of professional journals piled all over his place that he hadn't gotten to yet?

"It's okay." She took a sip of her wine. "In fact, I'm kind of glad you haven't. Somehow, it's easier to think of strangers reading it."

Stephen noted that she did not think of him as a stranger. He sat up a little straighter, remembering Tiffany rule #2. *Do not babble and act grateful for every little come-on.* "Perhaps we should order?" He said smoothly, nodding at the approaching waiter.

They made it through the entire meal chatting lightly about the weather, the city, and other innocuous subjects. Apparently, she then felt comfortable enough to answer the unspoken questions that kept flickering across his face.

She lowered her fork and folded her napkin. "Do you want to know what happened after I left your hospital?"

He laid his napkin down, too. "I do, honestly. I don't know why it feels so ... I've always wondered ..."

She reached across the table and patted his hand. "I'm flattered. No worries. I'm much better now." She sighed and leaned back in her chair. "You might actually find it amusing to know that when I first opened my eyes and saw your face, I thought, 'My God, they sent me a priest. Maybe I am going to die, after all.'"

The white streak was clearly visible in her now shoulder-length hair. Her brown eyes flickered with gold lights as she talked. Her mouth was thin, but there was strength to her nose. It was a good face, he decided.

"Do I have your attention, doctor?" She leaned toward him.

He was startled into meeting her eyes. "Stephen, please. And you have my complete attention. Go on."

"You are a brave man. Okay. When I opened my eyes and saw you standing there, I thought, hmm, one of those charming Irish boys, third son at least. I dated one, you see, so I know that in an Irish family the first son gets the business or farm, whatever. The second one is given over to the church, poor guy." She winked at him. "Only the third gets the luxury of going to college and choosing his career. So you see I knew you right away. I recognized your face." She flashed him an awkward smile that made his heart leap in his chest. "Now that I'm meeting you again, I would guess that you're a Virgo or a Capricorn, an earth sign. No fluffy Aquarian or smoldering Scorpio here." She took another sip of wine. "Some people think I'm kind of weird."

He was concentrating on not letting his mouth drop open.

Since he said nothing, she continued. "I figured you for a bookworm type, but from a rough-and-tumble family, the quiet one always trying to get noticed, and the kind who'd spend a lifetime denying that innocent face. You'd probably date a stripper, jump out of planes as a hobby, and play practical jokes that someone else always gets blamed for. But you are a kind and caring man, I saw it in your eyes then and I still do."

She paused. "That's why I decided in that instant not to talk to you." She picked up his hand and stroked his fingers lightly. "You felt dangerously sympathetic and I really wanted to die. God, that sounds so corny. I'd never write that. I was just so tired. Anyway," she glanced up, "I'll give you the abridged version. When I left you, I was taken to a lovely private hospital in Danville, Pennsylvania, where I spent the better part of a year working with a talented clinician named Susanna Powell, and I got over it."

"May I ask you something? I've always wanted to know if my instincts were correct."

"Sure. I have no secrets ... now."

Your hair?" He pointed to the white streak and took a breath. "I'd be willing to bet it's a family thing, hereditary. Maybe your mother has it?"

Her smile faded. "You *are* quick and almost right, but it's not my mother. It's my aunt Mimi. "Mimi" is actually her nickname. Her given name is Melissa Witherspoon. My parents died when I was a kid and I was raised by my two aunts, Mimi and Jane. I have no idea why my mother chose to name me after her oldest sister, because as far as I know they were never close. My mom was quite a bit younger. I do have some *issues* with Mimi, however. In fact, my clearest memory of that whole time was seeing her face, managing to show disgust and humiliation at the same time, when she came to your hospital to pick me up. Now, if you want the details, you'll just have to read the book. Or have dinner with me again." She hesitated. "But wait a minute, I believe I've explained why I remembered you despite the fact that we met so briefly. But how on earth did you recognize me some two years later?" She looked at him curiously.

Stephen was relieved. She had given him the perfect opening for what he needed to say. He took a deep breath. "I remembered you because seeing your ... lovely face, well, it literally changed my life."

Her eyes widened. "Wow, you do sneak up on a girl, don't you? That's quite a compliment."

He cleared his throat. "I'm not trying to impress you, it's just important to me that you know this." He paused, waiting for her to laugh or interrupt. She didn't. So he continued, "At Riverview I was stuck like a ... hamster in one of those exercise wheels, treating people who were never going to get better, the same people over and over, not making much of a difference."

He sighed. "I knew that I was doing it for the money, and it was a damned good job. But I needed a wakeup call." He glanced up at her then looked back down at the table. "You were it." She still sat silent.

"As soon as I saw you, I remembered that there were people who needed help but who had a chance to get better, out in the real world. I remembered what it was like to actually help someone. After that, I couldn't stay. I quit," he shrugged, "sold the Porsche I couldn't really afford, and started a practice where I could choose my own patients.

I also volunteer at a psych center that works with troubled kids." He smiled solemnly. "I feel like I actually make a difference now. Some of my patients go on to live relatively normal lives or what passes for normal around here."

She squeezed his hand and he could have sworn there were tears in her eyes. That's when the boy from the Bronx began to fall in love.

CHAPTER THREE

Melissa strolled into the maze of cubicles in the newspaper office and threw down her leather bag. One more story about farmers markets or local Going Green projects and she was going to puke. She had to get to work on her follow-up novel, that's all there was to it. She had been strangely unproductive ever since, well, Stephen.

Looking back on it eighteen months later, it seemed inevitable to Melissa. She felt as if no conscious decision had ever been made, as if some invisible hand had been pushing her along. They'd moved in together after six months and had shared the apartment for over a year now. She even loved his large, loud family. Not that they didn't fight once in a while. She had found Stephen to be a stronger, more stubborn man than he had at first seemed once you got beyond his compassion and ability to listen. She lost her temper, ranted and raved on occasion, and he was unfazed. As if she had the right. As if it was okay.

It was a ridiculously attractive quality in a man and one she had not encountered before. She had lately wondered if it was this comfortable domesticity that had prevented her from getting on with her second book. All that stuff about creative types needing to have pathetic tortured private lives or something like that.

There were several messages on her phone on the desk which surprised her. Anyone who knew her had her cell number. She pushed the buttons and listened.

"Melissa, sweetie, it's Aunt Jane."

She snatched up the receiver and took it off speaker phone. When she had listened to it several times, she threw down the phone, grabbed her bag, and bounded out the door. While tossing clothes into her suitcase, she called her cousin, Magee, who was one of the only people, other than Stephen, who could possibly understand what it meant for Melissa to return to Sylvan Mills.

A few years ago, Melissa, Magee, and their third cousin, Madison, had found each other through the internet. They had also discovered that each had the "gift", or as some called it, the "curse" of the Witherspoon women.

The cousins were descendents of a long line of Witherspoon women whose healing powers had once been strong enough to earn them rope burn necklaces. When they had gotten tired of being persecuted and treated as social outcasts, the women practiced their arts less and less. Gradually, their abilities diminished until only an unreliable possibility rather than a certain skill remained. Melissa had found a word, clairsentience, which seemed to come close to what Witherspoon women experienced when they felt another person's pain. It was comforting to have a name for the skill that had further complicated her already-challenged life.

Only one female in each family line was so gifted these days. Of the three sisters, only Mimi had it, which Melissa found ironic because either Jane or Emily would have been so much more suited to using it. When it had fallen to Mimi to explain it to Melissa, she had done her duty but made sure to pepper the explanation and demonstration with warnings not to use it.

Now that Melissa had met her Witherspoon cousins, they had been able to discuss how this ability affected them and how all three struggled to try to have normal lives and not to be defined by their inherited trait.

Melissa had bitten her tongue to keep from pointing out that not using it hadn't seemed to work out all that well for Mimi, who was feared and avoided and alone except for the devoted Jane. How much worse could her life have gotten if she had healed someone now and then? But Melissa had learned quickly to keep most of her thoughts to herself. It was possible, she guessed, that Mimi thought being a consummate social pariah was a good thing.

While Mimi's warnings had kept Melissa from even attempting to utilize her gift until she was well into college, she would surely be annoyed to know that Melissa had not taken her advice to let it lay dormant forever. The push/pull between being afraid and the inherent urge to use it was a constant strain on Melissa. This gift, whatever it was, would not be ignored.

Magee and Madison had shared similar stories. Each had situations arise in their lives that gave them no choice but to help.

When Magee came on the line she sounded harried and breathless. "Hello?"

"Hi cuz, sorry, I must be catching you at a bad time. You sound like you're out of breath."

"Mel! No problem, I'm just getting in a car heading up to Hartford for a hearing in Family Court. Is something wrong?"

After her marriage to Rick Ryder, rock star, and the birth of her son, Ryan, Magee had gone to work for a dynamic young female lawyer who specialized in child advocacy law. Magee loved the job and, with the encouragement of her family, was working on her law degree with hopes of eventually joining the firm as a partner.

"I'm sorry, really, I shouldn't bother you."

"No this is perfect, I have at least an hour car ride. Rick insists that I have a driver take me when I go any distance on business. Truth I very rarely go anywhere alone anymore, one of the perks or downsides, not sure which it really is, of being married to a superstar. Don't you ever tell him I called him that or I'll never hear the end of it. Okay, enough about me ... I haven't heard from you in quite a while. So what's going on?"

"Well, I told you all about my aunt Mimi, who raised me after my parents died?"

"Sure. She was my grandmother's cousin, although until I met you I had never heard of Mimi or Jane."

"Right. Well, I just got a call from Aunt Jane that Mimi is dying and she wants me to come home. I'm packing now and plan to leave in a few minutes. I just needed to talk to someone who would understand how difficult this is for me. As I told you, Mimi made my life a living hell when I was growing up in her house. I always said I'd never go back until she was dead. I was so mad when she forced me to go to college in New York."

"How many years has it been?"

"Eight."

"That's a long time, Mel. Maybe things have changed. Maybe you and Mimi can make your peace with each other before it's too late. As far as I'm concerned, it's about you living with yourself knowing that you tried to do the right thing. You know what I'm trying to say?"

"Yeah, I do. And you're right." Melissa nodded to herself. "After all, I was just a kid back then and I'm grown up now so I need to act like a grown up and take care of this. Sorry to sound so lame." She added, "I don't know what I'd do without you and Madison."

"Right back at ya, sweetie."

"I should get going then. I'll call as soon as I can to let you know what's happening, Mags, and thanks again."

"Be sure you do. Take care, Mel. Love you." And the phone went dead.

An hour later, Melissa and her vintage Mustang were on the road. She was halfway across New Jersey when she called to leave Stephen a voicemail.

As soon as she heard his voice on the recording, his face filled her mind. The soft sandy brown hair falling over his forehead; the gold-rimmed glasses that he pushed back up on his nose all the time; the round green eyes behind those glasses that seemed to focus only on you; the half-smile that always hovered at the edges of his mouth. He had the tall, lanky but solid body of an ex-athlete. His psychology practice and volunteer work at the clinic didn't allow time for much more than an occasional jog or pickup basketball game in the park, but he still looked pretty damned good at 6'2" and 190 lbs. What made him even sexier was that he had absolutely no idea how handsome and smart he actually was. And he loved her—weird and unlovable Melissa Sullivan! The truth was that things had been going so well, it was freaking her out.

Maybe this trip to Sylvan Mills would help her sort things out before he proposed and she managed to say or do the wrong thing and screw her life up completely. *Stop thinking and drive*, she chided herself. She thought about Sylvan Mills, her home town for what it was worth—one movie theater, one drug store, at least half a dozen bars ... and Daniel. It surely hadn't changed, no matter what Stephen said. But she could hear him in her head — *People don't freeze in place until we come back, Melissa, even if you want them to. They go on with their lives.*

Melissa pushed her head out the window, inhaled the fresh air, and exhaled Stephen's words into the wind. She downshifted the Mustang off the exit and concentrated on the winding back roads flanked by picture postcard farms.

Sylvan Mills was only a five-hour drive from New York City, but was, in many ways, a world away. She eased into a parking space across the street from One Witherspoon Lane. *Welcome back to small-town America, Melissa.* No meters, no signs, no alternate parking, and no circling the block waiting for a spot to open up. She sat for a minute or two, adjusting to being there, staring at the house.

The large Victorian on the top of the hill was outlined by the full moon, making it look even more intimidating than it was in the daylight. By the glow of the streetlight, she could still see the crack near the bottom of her old bedroom window where Daniel's rock had missed the frame that one time. They had tiptoed around for days, but her Aunt Mimi had never noticed. And if Aunt Jane did, she kept it to herself. As an objective adult, she could admire the gingerbread trim, the wide porch, and stained glass windows. But it had seemed like going from the gingerbread house to the wicked witch's castle when she had been an orphaned 11-year-old.

She was shivering. Her room was probably still that God-awful pink. She felt her pulse quicken and a cold sweat coming on. She whispered her personal mantra: "All will be well and will be well. All will be well and will be well." She had typed those lines over and over on her little portable typewriter when she came here to live and it became her source of strength in difficult situations ever since. She grabbed her water bottle and gulped down half of it. Maybe she should find a place to sleep and come back tomorrow. It might be easier to face in the daylight.

"Melissa?" Jane Witherspoon called as she flipped on the outside light and stepped onto the porch, drying her hands on her ever-present apron and peering through the twilight. "Melissa? Is that you?"

She had, of course, forgotten how little traffic there was in this town. People still looked out the window when a car whose sound was unfamiliar went by. They could sit in front of the TV, hear a truck go down the street, look at a watch, and say, "There goes Eddie, doin' the night shift this week."

She took a deep breath and opened the car door. *Think about what Magee said, you need to face this.* She stepped out of the car and waved. *You're a big girl, Mel. Just put one foot in front of the other and smile.*

Jane Witherspoon bounced up and down on her toes as she waited for Melissa to come up the porch steps, and then pulled her into the house. "Now, isn't that just like you to show up and not even call first? But I don't know why I'm surprised. You were always such an impulsive little thing."

Melissa bent down to hug her aunt.

"Jane, what is going on down there? Who's calling at this hour?"

Melissa glanced at her watch: 9:30. How could she have forgotten? According to Mimi rules, it was indecent to disturb one in one's home after dark without a formal invitation. She started up the stairs.

"It's Melissa."

"Well, la-di-da. And to what do we owe this honor?" The nasal voice echoed down the hall.

Melissa's good intentions quickly retreated into a simple resolve not to lose her temper.

Mimi's eyes glittered in the dim light of her bedroom's antique lamp. "Well, since I'm not dead yet, you might as well sit down." Seeing Jane's plump face, softer and gently sagging, yet so familiar and not greatly changed, had not prepared Melissa for her first glimpse of Mimi. Her long, thin face showed the signs of having endured years of illness and the ravages of time, and Melissa had to fight to keep the shock off her face. Mimi sat ramrod straight against her pillows, brown eyes sharp, voice still crisp with authority. But lines of pain carved into the pale face signaled the battle being fought with the disease eating her up from the inside and her always flawless ivory skin had a faint yellow tinge to it now.

Jane stepped out from behind Melissa. "Mimi, please, you be nice now. She's come all this way and everything. The kettle's on." Melissa sat down on the edge of a high-backed tapestry chair by the bed.

"Then bring us tea, Jane. And you'd better make up Melissa's room, if she's to get any sleep tonight," Mimi ordered.

Jane turned for the door.

Still treating her like a damned servant. "Just a minute." Melissa felt a small sharp pain as her fingernails dug into her palms. "I should just go to a hotel. It's late, I didn't call, and I don't want to be any trouble."

Jane looked wide-eyed from one to the other. "Oh, honey, please, it's no bother."

"Don't use that tone with me, young lady. Go to a hotel? Indeed. Wouldn't that be the talk of the county by morning!" Mimi sniffed.

Again, Jane started to move, but Melissa shook her head. *I will not buy into this. She can't make me.*

"I can make up the room myself, Aunt Jane," she said firmly. "Maybe I'll just do that now since it's late anyway and we'll talk tomorrow."

Mimi dismissed Jane with a final flick of her hand. "The woman is making tea. I am sure you will extend her the courtesy of staying put until it's served." She inhaled sharply and bent forward slightly as a stabbing pain hit her, then fought it off with an impatient shake of the head. She lay back against her pillows and looked intently at her niece. "Well, we all know I'm dying. What about you? You look well enough. Still living with that doctor?"

Melissa realized she was leaning forward with her arms folded defensively across her chest and deliberately pushed herself back against the chair cushion, placing her hands in her lap. *Don't go there. Just answer the question.* "Yes."

"I don't see a ring on that finger."

I'm living in sin. Deal with it. "I'm very happy with things the way they are for the time being, but I appreciate your concern," Melissa answered with controlled calm.

"Don't patronize me, girl." The gaunt face stretched into a smug smile. "I'm glad to hear that you're so happy, seeing as how Daniel MacBride has finally set the date, so I hear. But I suppose you knew that."

Melissa blinked once. "Of course."

"I figured you were in touch with Ellen MacBride. Then I suppose you also know she had a heart attack a few days ago." Mimi went off on a coughing jag and then took a deep breath. "Ah, there you are. Took you long enough, woman, can't you see the girl's tired? Pour, Jane."

Melissa accepted her cup grimly. Her aunt had always advocated horehound as "good for one's constitution." She sipped the bitter liquid as she and her aunt volleyed back and forth. Finally, after an exhausting half hour, she was instructed to kiss the papery, yellow cheek and allowed to take her leave. She and Jane tiptoed out. Melissa collapsed against the wall of the downstairs entry, holding her stomach.

Jane clucked her sympathy. "God bless you, child. I can't believe you actually drank that terrible stuff."

"What?" Melissa stared. "You didn't?"

"Lord, no, it's disgusting." Jane held up a handkerchief stained a muddy brown. "I blot up some to make her think I'm sipping. And I've had to replace a few houseplants, believe me. Join me for a real drink?"

Melissa managed a grin. "You're a wonder, Aunt Jane, you know that? But I don't think I could get anything else down right now."

After they had made up Melissa's bed and brought in her bag, Jane sat down heavily on the bed next to her niece, knowing just as she always had, when Melissa needed to talk.

In response to the hesitant question, Jane said gently, "Honey, I wish she hadn't told you about Daniel's mother. It was just unkind, your first night home and all. You'd have found out soon enough. Ellen MacBride had a heart attack last Thursday, and I'm sorry to say she's still at Community. But she's doing fine from what I've heard. You can go see her first thing, so don't you fret." She gave Melissa's leg a comforting pat. "I'm glad you're home, sweetie." She left the room, closing the door softly behind her.

Melissa looked around the familiar room. Memories from every object: the desk, the stuffed chair, the twin bed, wistfully clung to her. This place made her feel angry, stupid, and tired, it always had. *Christ, I hate pink.* In those days after her parents died, she was too shattered to protest the color, but now she wondered why she hadn't ever asked to have it redone. No, she didn't wonder. She had learned hard fast lessons in reality when she came to this house. It was best to ask for as little as possible and expect to get about half of that.

Suddenly the voice in her head called out to her. *Ellen.* She tried to ignore it; she was tired. But the voice in her head wouldn't stop. *Ellen.* It was her Witherspoon nagging, this voice hammering at her, she needed to see Ellen. *Now.* Melissa sighed, knowing that she always regretted ignoring it. She had learned the hard way to trust her instincts, so she grabbed her keys and let herself out the front door.

CHAPTER FOUR

Mimi heard the front door close but that's not what kept her awake. By noon tomorrow, every wretched busybody in this town would know she was here. People had little business of their own so they constantly had their noses in everybody else's. She would be getting a phone call, likely first thing in the morning.

"You promised me." The man would say reasonably. "You know how important it is to me. This is a very inopportune time for this issue to arise."

And she would remind him that nothing had changed. "Anything happens to me prematurely, or to Melissa, and there are very reliable people holding evidence to make sure all your ugly little secrets come home to roost. All you have to do is leave her alone and let me die in peace."

That would hit the mark. He would likely hesitate then give her one last reminder—"I want her out of this town and the sooner the better."

Mimi sighed and reached over to her bedside table, pulling her younger sister's picture from the drawer. *Emily*. Had it really been fifteen years since she'd placed it in there? Since she had left and everything had gone wrong? The mist that blurred her eyes surprised her and she leaned back against the pillows.

She was a silly, soft-hearted girl, Emily was, so delighted to take the baby Mimi placed in her arms. She and that husband of hers had done a good job raising the girl. Even when Emily foolishly named her Melissa after her older sister, no one suspected, no one cared. It was simply construed as a way to restore her to her sister's good graces and the family fortune. Mimi had been able to use that contrived alienation to keep the girl at a safe distance. She saw to it that they had what they needed.

Then they went and got themselves killed. What was to be done? She unconsciously smoothed the sheet across her legs, just as she had smoothed her skirt that day as she waited for that woman to bring her. Annette Hayden was it? That's right, the wife of the newspaper editor, she was the social worker who brought the girl back to her. Was this God's vengeance for her immoral behavior? Should she have aborted the child the way Garrett wanted her to? She clenched her fists. *No!* She had hidden the pregnancy, she had given birth in another state, and she had done all the work. It was for her to say.

But Melissa's father, with his lofty political ambitions, had harassed her constantly; angry because she would not simply get rid of the baby, worried that someone might see the resemblance. Year after year, she'd held him at bay through sheer strength of will, keeping Melissa as far from him as possible in a town this size, which was also the county seat and the jumping-off point for Garrett's career.

Finally, Melissa graduated high school and Mimi could relax. It was a perfectly natural thing for a child to go off to school. So she'd forced Melissa off to college in New York and, of course, Melissa hated her for it. It was harder than she had expected to let her go. But at least she was safely off his radar, out of his sight.

Until Jane, bless her innocent soul, asked Melissa to come back to Sylvan Mills! Always trying to help with no thought of the consequences—that was Jane. Mimi was sick and tired, and had hoped to slide easily into the restful sleep she truly believed she had earned, but not yet.

One sister had forced her into battle by dying; the other had sent her back to it by good intentions. God must be laughing at her yet again. She heard Him mocking her all those years ago and she heard Him now. She fully grasped the irony, but failed to see the humor.

CHAPTER FIVE

The only hospital in the county was apparently not concerned about security. When Melissa whooshed through the automatic doors, she found the reception desk empty and the security guard asleep in a lounge chair, a jumbo coffee cup on the floor beside him. Melissa strode past him like she knew where she was going. As she rode up to the second floor in the almost silent elevator, she couldn't help but think that this was as easy as it looked in those movies where the killer came to finish off the witness in his hospital bed. The ones where you never believe they could get away with it. A wry smile flickered across her tired face. She slipped down the dimly lit hallway and through the swinging door marked 204.

It was the right room; she was sure without looking at the name on the chart hanging at the foot of the bed. The familiar black curls, now sprinkled with some gray, tumbled across the pillow. Yet the figure in the bed seemed much smaller than she remembered, outlined by white linens and dwarfed by the big metal bed.

Something swept through Melissa, unfamiliar and uncomfortable. As the lone survivor of the accident that had killed her parents, Melissa liked to think she had done her time with guilt and had pretty much given up on shame. Yet, as she sank into the chair next to the bed that held her friend and surrogate mother, something awfully close, unfamiliar and uncomfortable, nagged at her.

What could she possibly say to Ellen? She had meant to come see her; she had meant to call, she really had. Something kept her from it. Maybe there were things she didn't want to know, was afraid to hear. As Stephen said, if she didn't find out differently, then Sylvan Mills remained frozen in time, waiting for her to come back and get it right. She sighed. Living with a psychologist could be rather disconcerting. She hated it when Stephen was right, and he was usually right.

All she had managed was a short, cheery note now and then, a Christmas card, all signed with her bold "Love, M." Ellen had no way of knowing how many times Melissa had desperately needed to hear that soft Irish lilt telling her everything would be all right. Or how often, in the silence of her lonely dorm room or her small apartment, she had relived all those wonderfully hectic and noisy MacBride family dinners.

Melissa tried to be honest, at least with herself, but the truth smacked her in the face as she sat next to the woman who had deserved so much better from her. She hadn't called or visited. She had just walked away. It didn't really matter that she truly never meant to, that was how it played out, wasn't it?

Enough. Melissa raised her head and composed herself. With any luck, she wouldn't have to explain, at least not tonight. Ellen seemed to be sleeping deeply and Melissa sincerely hoped she had been given a sleep aid of some type. She laid a gentle hand on the pale, freckled arm, said a quick prayer for protection, and opened herself to the woman's physical condition.

Jane was wrong. She tried not to gasp as she pulled away. Or maybe she had simply been doing her glass-half-full act for Melissa's benefit. Ellen was weak and there was damage to her heart. Melissa sank into the chair next to the bed to let the dizziness and pain in her chest subside. She took several deep breaths. *Come on,* she pushed herself, *just do it. Don't stop to think. You owe her.* And with that voice inside her making the decision, she was ready. The trouble was that she was never sure what she might be able to do.

Melissa peeked out into the hallway and listened for a moment. All clear, nothing but quiet murmurs from the nurses' station at the other end of the hall.

Closing the door quietly, she pulled a chair up close behind her. She raised her hands over Ellen's body and said a few prayers for self-protection. She closed her eyes as she gently placed them on the narrow chest and heat cycled through her own body. Daggers flew into her chest and her heartbeat pounded in her ears. She fell backward, hard, into the chair. She panted and then drew in a few deep, cleansing breaths until the pain began to ease. She helped herself to the carafe of water on the bedside stand. She said another prayer and, battling every instinct of self-preservation, stood up to do it again. It was always harder the second time. Her body seemed to know what was coming and didn't want to expose itself to more pain.

She moved slowly, knowing that she was tiring quickly. When she was almost out on her feet, she forced out one last rush of her own strength, pushing waves of it through her splayed fingers into Ellen. That was all she had; it would have to do for now.

It felt like she'd been there for hours, but it was only a little past midnight when Melissa stumbled out into the darkness and drove back to the house. She was asleep almost before her head hit Jane's pressed rose-scented pillowcase.

CHAPTER SIX

Back in New York, Stephen had been stunned by the voicemail. When Melissa didn't pick up on her cell phone, he cancelled his last session and raced home. She was already gone. He paced back and forth, muttering furiously. Why hadn't she given him a chance to go with her? Did she have any idea what she was doing? What a minefield that town, that house, that woman, was for her? Why didn't she trust him? When his phone rang, he grabbed it.

"Mel?"

"No, darling, it's Tiffany."

He sighed.

"Well, thanks a bunch. I just wondered if we were still on for dinner."

"What?"

Her voice rose in indignation. "Dinner. You promised. *Chez Pierre*. What is wrong with you?"

He told her.

"Well, listen, buster; it took me a month to get this reservation so you're coming anyway. Be there at 8. We'll talk then." She slammed the phone shut. Tiffany had been listening to Stephen talk about Melissa for months. So she had decided to use it as a means to try out every expensive restaurant she could get them into. Great food was her biggest weakness and even better when someone else was footing the bill.

So, at 8 sharp, Tiffany was ensconced at a small table, caressing the burgundy and ivory menu with reverence. *Chez Pierre*. She had starved herself through lunch and already checked the dinner menu on their web site. *Bouillabaisse Marseillesse*. The syllables rolled off h tongue and made her mouth water. Where was Stephen? She was totally ready to strap on the feedbag.

She had polished off most of the bread basket by the time he flopped into the chair opposite her. At least he was wearing a suit even though he looked a bit disheveled compared to his usual dapper self. She reached for the wine menu; it might be a two-bottle evening.

"She's gone, Tiff, she left me a voicemail. She went back to that town in Pennsylvania. Can you believe that? She takes off just like that and she leaves me a freakin' voicemail." His hands raked through his sandy hair.

"Hello there. Nice to see you. You look great. Hi. Nice to see you, too. Thanks." She ran her red-tipped fingers through her long blond hair and glared at him with her intensely blue eyes.

He pushed his gold-rimmed glasses higher up on his nose, and threw both hands straight up in the air. "I know what this is. She's testing me, trying to drive me off so she can say, 'I told you so. No one stays. No one can be trusted. The only person I can count on is me.'"

"For chrissakes, stop waving your hands like that. You're not conducting an orchestra." She leaned forward and hissed at him. "This is a nice place. Now sit up straight and take a deep breath."

He picked up his napkin and noticed a passing waiter, white linen cloth draped over his arm, crimson rose in his black lapel. "Dear God, this place looks ..."

"You betcha. If I have to listen to you go on about Melissa all night, it's worth four-stars, buddy, so suck it up."

He eyeballed the menu and his mouth fell open. She shot him her "don't you dare" look.

His breath came out in a long sigh. "I don't get it. Things have been going so well these last few months. But she took off on her own without giving me a chance to help her prepare for this."

Tiffany wondered, not for the first time, why she continued to let Stephen be a part of her life. *Now there's a topic for my next therapy session.* But here she was, getting a first class dinner out of it at least, while Stephen, in his methodical way of dealing with everything, relived the ongoing agony of his relationship with Melissa. She kicked her shoes off under the table and signaled the waiter to refill the bread.

"She has this ... fixation ... on that town. She thinks she can go back to being 11 again and make it come out with a happier ending." He shook his head. "That won't happen, Tiff. She's going to get hurt."

Tiffany caught a glimpse of that faraway look in his eyes. When the waiter returned with another basket of warm baguette, she glanced over at Stephen, and then shrugged up at him. "A bottle of your best burgundy and you better have a backup."

Back to the menu. Ooh, she'd better order the chocolate raspberry soufflé with her entrée because it needed extra prep time. It was their showcase dessert. Tiffany sighed in contentment. What was that saying—it's an ill wind that doesn't do somebody some good? *Thank you, Melissa, wherever you are.*

Tiffany looked around the room. She loved the color scheme in this place. *Do I dare paint my dining room red?* She sighed, and then realized she didn't have to please anyone but herself. *Go for it, already. Wait a minute, I signed up for that singles cruise, didn't I? That should be fun.* As she picked up her wineglass, she noticed that she'd chipped a nail. *Ah, nuts.*

The motion brought Stephen back to the present.

"You know, she thinks this town has just been sitting there, waiting for her to come back. She's wrong. If I had told her that, she'd think I was lying because I didn't want her to go. But it's going to be ugly, Tiff, there's no way this works out for her. Every instinct I have says it's going to be a disaster." He drained his wine glass.

He continued to ramble on in the same vein until Tiffany finished her meal and was ready for dessert. She slapped Stephen's hand. "Hey, you, want the crème brulee or cheesecake? I already ordered the soufflé. Never mind, crème brulee it is." Stephen nodded and started paying attention to the filet mignon he didn't remember ordering.

Tiffany sipped her cappuccino contentedly. *Could I make crème brulee at home? I'd have to get those little dishes, the whatchamacallits, at The Kitchen Cupboard? Hmm.*

Cooking lessons, now there's a way to get a guy. Maybe if I learned to cook more than eggs and pasta. Comfort foods like meatloaf and pot roast. Geez that sounded so ... whatever.

Cooking lessons—there has to be some place in the city. Guys take these lessons too, right? So, even if I sucked at it, maybe I'd meet a guy who actually liked to cook ... "Ramekins"!

Stephen stopped and stared at her, as did the couples at the three neighboring tables. She blushed then grinned at him, "Sorry."

She ate most of both desserts while Stephen picked at his filet. Waving his fork in her general direction, he continued his *soliloquy*. The word had come to her during the salad course.

He stopped to sip his coffee and suddenly reached over and patted her hand. "You know what I love most about you, Tiff? You're such a good listener."

She smiled.

Just then, a white jacket appeared beside the table. Tiffany looked up at a dazzling smile beneath cool blue eyes with dark hair edging from under the chef's hat.

"Madame, you are liking my soufflé?" He murmured with an adorable French accent.

Tiffany swallowed. "Yes, very much, thank you." She recovered enough to check his left ring finger. *Oh yes, thank you, Jesus.* She cleared her throat. "It was the perfect ending to a perfect meal. You have a gift."

He gently picked up her hand and kissed it. "You do me great honor." She would have sworn he looked at her ring finger too. "Perhaps you will come again?"

Tiffany remembered to breathe. "Ah well, I don't, I mean ..." She looked to Stephen for help.

"Of course." Stephen said firmly. "And I'd like to bring my girlfriend. She'd love it too."

Tiffany felt herself coloring slightly.

The chef nodded. "Ahh, then perhaps mademoiselle will return as my guest." He reached into his pocket and pulled out a card and laid it gently next to Tiffany's plate. "I am Francois."

"Tiffany."

"Oui. A beautiful name for a beautiful woman." He bowed slightly and was gone.

Wide-eyed, she looked at Stephen, who chuckled. "I know, you're in love."

She smiled broadly and exhaled. "Well, he sure is hot. Ooolala." She picked up the card and put it in her purse without looking at it. She discreetly glanced around to see if Francois was stopping at other tables but the white coat was gone.

Stephen reached over and took a bite of the soufflé. "Wow."

"How can you think about food at a time like this?" She demanded.

He choked; she handed him his water glass.

"Okay, my friend, let's wrap this up. I have to work tomorrow." She laid her napkin on the table and frowned at him. "Here's the bottom line. You're being such a Capricorn."

"Huh?"

"You know, I've told you before. You've decided she's the one and now you'll hang in there as long as it takes."

"It feels like I'm hanging on for dear life." He wiped his mouth and replaced the napkin in his lap.

Tiffany forced herself to ignore the pain in his eyes and got straight to the point. "Listen, remember that silly little poem thing that says—if you love something, set it free? If it doesn't come back, hunt it down and kill it?" She waited that second or two for the horrified look the joke deserved. "Just kidding! The saying is: If it doesn't come back, it was never really yours."

He stared at her.

"Haven't you ever heard of reverse psychology, doctor? Women are perverse creatures. She knows you love her. So stop clinging. Let her go, Stephen, and see if she comes back to you."

He shook his head. "I don't think I can do that."

Tiffany was not surprised. "That's what I figured. Pay the check." She beckoned to the waiter and pointed to Stephen's half-eaten filet. "I'll need this wrapped to go, please."

CHAPTER SEVEN

Melissa awoke the next morning to the smell of breakfast cooking and wondered for just a minute where she was. If she and Stephen wanted breakfast, they usually walked down to the corner café.

Aunt Jane! She jumped up and threw her clothes on, hurried into the kitchen. She and Jane laughed and chatted through bacon, eggs and toast, then Melissa took a tray upstairs for Mimi. She forced herself to chat for ten minutes or so before bouncing down the stairs and out the door.

This time, Ellen was awake when she walked into the room.

She exclaimed, "Sweet Mother o' God! Melissa! I cannot believe I'm seein' ya, girl. Get over here and let's have a look at ya." Ellen made a circular motion weakly with her right hand.

Melissa raised her arms and did a slow modeling turn.

"Ya're just as lovely, girl, as I thought ya'd be. But ya're still too thin. Now give us a kiss," Ellen said in her Irish lilt that remained even though she'd lived in the States since she was a young child.

"My dahling Ellen, don't you know, one simply cannot be too thin." She bent down and kissed the pale cheek. "I've missed you." She gently caressed Ellen's curls. "How are you, really?"

"Better now that ya're here. Janie called this mornin' to tell me you was back. Think she was scared I'd have another heart attack but in truth seein' ya makes me feel much better."

A nurse arrived to check on Ellen. While she tended to IVs and monitors, she still managed to give Melissa a stern once-over. "Miss, visiting hours don't start for another hour and are restricted to immediate family."

"Aw, lighten up, Betty. 'Tis Melissa Sullivan. Ya went to school with 'er, doncha recognize 'er?" Ellen replied with a smile.

"Omigod." The nurse's face softened. "I read your book. I wish I had it with me. I'd ask you to sign it."

Melissa blushed and shook her hand. "Thanks. Good to see you, but I guess I should leave."

"I'm sorry but breakfast is coming." The nurse's words were punctuated by the sounds of squeaky carts and rattling plastic trays in the hall.

"It's okay. I got in late last night so I'm kind of wiped out. But I wanted to get a look at Ellen myself first thing to see how she's doing." Melissa turned back to Ellen and squeezed her hand. "Listen, you've got to get out of here. We have lots of catching up to do and you know how I hate hospitals."

Ellen squeezed back. "Me, too."

"I'm going now. But I'll be back. I'm staying with the aunts." She crossed her eyes and turned toward the door.

"Missy."

The old nickname stopped her in her tracks. She turned back to Ellen and said, "No one calls me that anymore."

"I do." Ellen's chin tilted upward in stubborn mode.

Melissa smiled. "Well, all right then."

"I thank ya for cumin'."

The unexpected quiver in Ellen's voice brought tears to Melissa's eyes. All she could do was nod before fleeing to the nearest ladies' room to pull herself together. Inside, a petite young woman struggled with a stroller and a squirming baby.

Melissa was forced to pull her thoughts away from Ellen. "May I help?" she asked with a warm smile.

The woman raised her head. "Melissa? Melissa Sullivan?" Then she laughed at the confused expression on Melissa's face.

"I wouldn't expect you to remember me. I'm Annie Harrison, Annie Harrison MacBride now. I was a couple years behind you in school. I recognized you, of course, from the book and all."

"Oh, my goodness!" Melissa responded to the name. "So you're married to one of the twins, I'm guessing?"

"That's right, I'm married to Tom. Tim's in the service out in California right now." The baby wailed. Annie kissed his little red cheek and murmured soothing noises.

As he quieted down, playing with her necklace, she spoke again to Melissa. "And this is Tommy. He's been running a fever and his pediatrician said to bring him over here. We've been in the waiting room for over an hour and I really have to go." She blushed and looked toward the bathroom stall.

"I'll take him." Melissa gave the baby an encouraging smile.

"Thank you so much. I won't be a minute." She handed the baby to Melissa and ducked into a stall.

"Okay, little guy. Let's have a look at you." As soon as she took the hot little body in her arms, she sighed. *Hospitals.* She had more reason to avoid them than most people. Should she help the sick babies or the old folks in needless pain? She always left feeling inadequate and unhappy with whatever choice she had made.

But there was no help for it with those big blue eyes staring solemnly at her, the warm little legs wrapped around her waist. She was a bit worn out this morning but he was small, how much could it hurt? Melissa placed a hand on his forehead and then ran it over his head lightly, searching out the source of his fever. *Aha, left ear.* She sat him down on the counter, placed a hand over his hot ear, and invoked a quick, silent prayer for protection. As a wave of heat flew into her ear and gave her an instant headache, she groaned involuntarily.

There was a flushing sound, the door to the stall opened and Annie came rushing out. "Is everything all right?"

Melissa forced a smile. "Fine. Fine." She handed the baby over. "Either I'm totally fascinating or he may be feeling better."

Annie felt his forehead, "Omigod. I can't believe it." The baby gave his mother a big toothless grin as drool ran down his chin.

"Won't you be relieved when he can talk?" Melissa chuckled.

"Absolutely. Well, I gotta get back to the waiting room. Thank you so much." She pulled a baby wipe from the diaper bag, expertly swiped it across Tommy's face, and tucked him back into the stroller. "I hope we get to see you again while you're in town." Then the door closed.

Melissa washed her hands and looked into the mirror. *Thank God the baby couldn't talk.* Her headache was already fading. It had definitely been worth it. The little guy was Daniel's nephew! Her heart pounded as she realized she might run into him anytime now. It was a small town. She heard Stephen's voice in her head. *And how does that make you feel?*

CHAPTER EIGHT

"Hey, mom, guess who's back in town?" Betty said in a low voice on the phone at the nurse's station. Her mother called her sister, who called her best friend, who was a neighbor of Annette Hayden's. Less than half an hour after Melissa walked into Ellen's hospital room, Annette's phone rang.

She was standing at her kitchen sink, coffee mug in hand, watching the birds in her back yard. Melissa Sullivan was back in town. *Melissa Sullivan.* It was still painful to hear the name.

Over the years, Annette, as the county children's services agent, had dealt with some heartbreaking cases. Unwanted, neglected, abused kids, you name it, she had seen it. Ironically, Melissa, raised in a warm, loving home and then entrusted to the care of a wealthy family member, still felt like one of her failures.

July 22, 1996. Charlie called her and broke the news. Terrible accident, Rob and Emily Sullivan killed. She flew out of her office, raced to the hospital. The girl was sitting in the emergency room waiting area. When Annette called her name and reached out a hand to her, she had come home with her without saying a word.

By the time they got to the house, the phone was ringing and it didn't stop until she pulled the plug. Concerned citizens wanted to express their shock and dismay at the tragic accident that had claimed the lives of Rob and Emily Sullivan. Most callers felt compelled to share a personal story about the popular couple and then went on to convey their horror at the possibility that Mimi might become guardian of the child, even managing to air a few personal grievances against the "nasty old bitch, may she rot."

The next morning at the office, it was the same. Annette fielded as many calls as she could stand, and then ripped her phone cord out of the wall. She understood that there was a clear consensus that it was absurd to even think of turning Melissa over to Mimi "who shouldn't be trusted with a live plant, let alone a child." But she had not heard one constructive suggestion as to how to legally keep that from happening.

Even Mimi's own attorney voiced his regret but, like the rest of those to whom she had spoken, the bottom line was "the law is the law." Emily Sullivan had, for reasons beyond anyone's comprehension, named her oldest sister as the child's guardian and there was no basis to prove her unfit. What bothered Annette was that there wasn't a single soul in town who believed that she was fit, either.

Melissa was to be given over to Mimi to live in that monstrosity on Witherspoon Lane and Annette was the one who had to take her there. *This was just not the way it was supposed to work.*

She had almost quit over it. It didn't feel like the job Annette had made so many compromises for—feeding her boys pizza for dinner, doing laundry at midnight, turning her precious Bethany over to a sitter three afternoons a week, even enduring her husband's advice on working in the real world.

Before he retired, George Evans had decided she would be his replacement. He called her up and hooked her with his simple, inspiring description of the job: rescue hurt children and find them safe haven. *Safe haven* had stuck like a cupid's arrow in her mother's heart. She was extraordinarily qualified, not just by virtue of her degree in social work and her own three children, but because this town was her home, her parents' home, her grandparents' home. She was related to half the town and had gone to school with the rest. She knew which families needed a little help and which ones always had room for one more.

There was more to the job than that, of course. She wrestled daily with a temperamental computer, the unending stream of forms and reports, and supervisors who made long-distance decisions whose repercussions were hard to justify. When there were battles to be fought, she fought them and that was okay. The fact that she didn't need the job gave her an edge and she used it—for all the good that did Melissa.

It was just after noon when the call she had been dreading came. Annette listened in disgusted silence as Mimi Witherspoon, in her irritatingly pinched nasal voice, advised Annette that she had been working with her attorney to make the necessary funeral arrangements and had been considering her niece's situation. She suggested calmly that Melissa might be happier in a more traditional family setting like she was used to. When Annette did not respond, she cut to her usual bottom line. "We would expect to pay all expenses, of course."

Annette couldn't have agreed more but she couldn't bear to hear it. "You'll have to check with your attorney, Ms. Witherspoon. He has advised me that you are the child's legal guardian, according to the terms of your sister's will." She couldn't resist adding, "And believe me, if there was anything I could do to change that, I would," before slamming down the receiver. Feeling slightly nauseated, she ran to the ladies' room to wash up. But the reflection in the mirror of her frantically scrubbing her hands sent her rushing back to her desk, hands still dripping.

Ellen MacBride had called to offer Melissa a home. She hardly needed to say that she would treat Melissa as her own. The whole town knew Ellen had cried when she had given birth to her fourth boy. Annette's mind raced through the legalities: if Mimi was willing to let them file temporary change of guardianship papers, it could be done. She dialed Mimi's number, willing to eat a little crow if it got Melissa into the MacBride house.

But Mimi had been giving the matter some thought, and, of course, the girl belonged with family. Annette need not trouble herself any further. She would, please, bring the girl at one o'clock tomorrow. *Like a pizza or a piece of furniture,* Annette had thought bitterly.

That next morning, she had stood at her kitchen sink clutching her coffee mug, watching the ballet of the birds, big and small, that surrounded Charlie's birdfeeders in the backyard. He spent what little spare time he had stocking berries, suet, and seed, and filling the bath. At first, she resented that, wishing her husband would build her some new kitchen cabinets or learn to fix their cars, instead. But eventually she had learned to stop and savor the splashing of wings in sparkling water, the delicate pecking and choosing, the joyful chirping that told the rest of the birds in the neighborhood that food was there for the taking. She had come to see that the families of finches, jays, cardinals, and mourning doves, even the plain brown sparrows, did the same things she did: fought for their babies, struggled to keep them safe, and help them grow.

If she closed her eyes now, she could still feel her husband's warm arms wrapping around her, hugging her tightly just as they had all those years ago at the end of that horrible day. Her thoughts wandered back again...

"Mrs. Hayden?"

Annette started slightly as the clear voice broke the silence from the back seat of her car. "Yes, Melissa."

The girl cleared her throat. "I'd like to go home first."

Annette knew that this might happen. She turned around in the seat to see the child's face. "Oh, honey, I don't think ..."

"Just for a minute. Just to get my things." The golden-brown eyes showed the first flicker of emotion Annette had seen since the accident. "It won't take long."

Fingers raking her unruly red curls, Annette considered. "I'm not sure it's a good idea, Melissa. Mrs. Foster brought your suitcase."

"All she brought was my clothes. I need my stuff!" the girl protested.

It didn't seem too much to ask. She started the car with a sigh, looking at her watch. "We'll have to make it quick."

A surprised but pleased look fleeted across the long pale face. "It won't take long. I know what I want."

Annette's mind raced through numerous scenarios as she drove hard and fast down the country road. *What if Melissa became hysterical? What if she fainted? What if she refused to leave? Oh, God. This could be a really bad idea.* The girl was out of the car before she had turned off the engine.

Annette had followed her up the stairs of the small white farmhouse, the screen door slamming behind her. She found herself taking deep breaths as she looked at the worn sofa with its handmade afghan thrown over the back, the wooden farm table and chairs, the assortment of cows decorating the mantel and the bookshelves. There were ceramic cows, metal cows, cows of all colors.

She had followed Melissa to her room. Posters almost covered the lavender walls; a small electric typewriter sat in the middle of a purple desk. Melissa frantically pulled papers from the desk and threw them into a backpack. She grabbed a walkman off the desk and put it into the bag, tucked the typewriter under her arm, and marched straight out of the room. Annette had the feeling that she thought that she could only take what she herself could carry. She trailed behind her, trying to decide if it was good or bad that she showed so little reaction to the home she would never see again.

Melissa stopped in the living room and picked out a delicate porcelain purple cow from the fireplace mantle, tucked it gently into her backpack, turned, and walked out of the house, the screen door again slamming behind her. Annette found herself taking deep breaths as she closed the front door of the silent house and followed her to the car.

When they pulled up in front of Mimi's house, Annette noted the pallor of the girl's thin face, her brown eyes with golden specks catching the light, and the odd white streak in her soft brown hair, just at her part line on the right. She considered, and then swallowed, the inane things she wanted to say—Are you going to be okay? *Of course not.* Is there anything I can do? *Obviously not.*—as they stood looking at the Witherspoon house.

It had been an impressive mansion, surely, but years of neglect had grayed the white paint, weakened the black shutters, and torn off bits of the gingerbread here and there. The settling of the hilltop added the insult of making it crooked, and the sidewalk and steps leading to it tilted first one way and then the other. A crooked house on a crooked hill; by the general consensus, perfect for the slightly twisted Witherspoons, the locals said. Annette had been overwhelmed by a strong urge to grab the girl and drive away. As if she sensed that, Melissa had let go of her hand.

She placed her other things on the porch and took her suitcase from Annette. Then she looked Annette squarely in the eye. "Thank you for everything, Mrs. Hayden." With that dismissal, she resolutely rang the bell.

Within seconds, the door opened and Melissa and her things were taken inside. Then it closed with a firm click.

That was unacceptable. Annette shoved a finger hard against the button, needing a better ending to this day. Melissa opened the door and Annette almost wished she hadn't. The girl had looked at her with a compassionate understanding in her eyes that haunted Annette for months afterward. She couldn't even explain it to Charlie. It was a light going out, a look that had no place on the face of a child.

"I'm okay," the girl had said. Her eyes added, "I'm on my own now."

This time when the door closed, Annette, half blinded by tears she could no longer fight back, had made her way back to her station wagon, reminding herself again and again that she was a professional. She headed for home. She had her home to go to; but now the cozy farmhouse that had been Melissa's home would soon have a "For Sale" sign in the front yard.

She parked the car in the driveway and sat there for a few minutes. Then she went into the garage, put on the gloves, and hit the old punching bag until she felt better. Charlie had placed a vase of roses on the kitchen table for her. And better yet, he was waiting and didn't say a word, just opened his arms.

Good God, some days Annette had a hard time remembering her grandkids' names and yet she recalled that day with crystal clarity. She took a sip of the hot, rich liquid in her mug and sighed. *Charlie. God bless him.* He was gone three years already and still she missed him every day.

Annette continued her watch out the window where the birds splashed and sang. After Melissa left town, Ellen MacBride, one of her best friends and bridge partner, had shown her a few of the cheerfully scrawled notes from around the world with the big bold "M" at the bottom. She had kept her in her prayers all these years, almost convinced herself that Melissa was fine, she was grown up now, no permanent damage done from living with Mimi Witherspoon. But she knew that she wasn't fine. Annette had read the book.

CHAPTER NINE

Chief of Police Daniel MacBride strode down the hospital hallway, past the closed ladies' room door behind which Melissa was holding his nephew. His fiancé, Jennifer, quick-stepped to keep up while chattering on breathlessly about their upcoming wedding and honeymoon plans.

In her room, Ellen ignored the rubbery mass on her plate, euphemistically named a "healthy heart" egg white omelet, and pulled Melissa's book from her bedside drawer, opening it to the page with the turned-down corner:

> *Her latest conquest, an older man, loved games.*
> *He taught her how to give pleasure and how to*
> *find it. The word love just never came up. What*
> *they had was mutual satisfaction.*
>
> *When she met a young man whom she wanted*
> *to date, she knew she could tell him. He would*
> *stroke her arm and say lightly, "Ah, off you go*
> *then, love." It was still a wonder to her that there*
> *were no tears, no dramatic scenes, but then she*
> *felt the same way.*
>
> *Her heart was firmly enveloped in the tough*
> *scar tissue that had thickened and hardened each*
> *year. Such losses could barely scratch the*
> *surface. So, on she went, from one to another,*
> *and they simply didn't matter.*

When Jennifer came through the doorway, Ellen slammed the book shut.

"Mother MacBride, how are you?"

Ellen winced. Her eyes narrowed as they met Daniel's above Jennifer's head. He gave her a tense smile and a fast shake of the head before moving to stare out the window at the green, rounded Alleghenies. Jennifer touched Ellen's arm, her diamond ring catching the light, and Ellen twitched with an obvious effort not to pull away.

Jennifer glanced at Daniel, who seemed to be thoroughly fascinated by the view. She forced a smile. "How are you feeling today? You look much better, Mother MacBride."

"I'll thank ya not to call me that and I've told ya so before!" It came out sharper than Ellen intended. "I don't like it. My name is Ellen, for pity's sake."

The color rose in Jennifer's cheeks. "I'm sorry." Her glance fell to the book lying beneath Ellen's hand. "So it's her again. I should have known. If she had ever given a damn about you," her eyes flickered to Daniel's back, "about any of you, she wouldn't be living in New York now, would she?"

Ellen's eyes met hers with a look of distaste mixed with compassion.

"I've really tried to make you like me, Ellen, but I've just about had it." Jennifer flounced out of the room.

Daniel turned and looked at the closing door.

"She'll not go far, don't ya worry ya'rself," his mother said firmly.

"Ma!" He came to her bedside and looked down at her reproachfully.

"'Tis not that I don't want ya to get married an' have a family, son. I do, but just not with the likes of that one." Ellen answered.

Daniel sank into the chair beside the bed and answered in his usual patient way. "Ma, that's not fair and you know it. It's time for me to be getting on with it if I'm going to have a family. And you have to try to get along with Jen."

He grinned. "I'm not getting any younger, though you may be."

"Melissa's 'ere, son! She's cum home!" There was victory in her voice.

His head jerked up. "What?"

"She was 'ere this mornin'. She's stayin' with the aunts. She's lovely, too." Ellen sighed with pleasure and a hint of pride. She closed her eyes to rest for just a moment.

Daniel frowned and mentally cursed. He had figured his mother's dream would die a natural death, especially after he married Jen, and he'd never have to have the awkward conversation where he explained why he and Melissa together forever was just a dream. Not gonna happen.

Daniel knew the day Melissa left for college. She was crying, all right, and angry and scared, but he had seen something else in her eyes, too. Call it excitement or ambition. She was on her way to New York City and, even if he wasn't the sharpest tack in the box, he knew that day she'd probably never be back.

Yet he had waited, like a lovesick schoolboy or a goddamned fool, thinking that maybe after she graduated from college ... then after she had gone to the city ... then after she had written her book ... but the waiting was over. He was going to marry Jennifer, who had been waiting too and would never leave him.

The reality hit him like a ton of bricks. *Christ, Melissa Sullivan was back in Sylvan Mills.* He would have to deal with it and find a way to look her in the eye and pretend not to care. There were some in town, like his mom, who would be delighted; some others not so much, like Jennifer. But there were serious players in this town who would be very unhappy. Melissa could have no idea that she was stepping into a nest of rattlesnakes but he did. Daniel's stomach flipped as he realized he was going to have a lot to deal with over the next few days. He closed his eyes and sighed. *Melissa.*

CHAPTER TEN

Jennifer Murphy was seriously pissed off. She stormed out of the hospital and all but ran across the parking lot. Thank God she had driven herself. She fumbled with her keys, managing to drop them onto the pavement. She muttered an obscenity as she scooped them up, slammed herself down onto the seat while yanking the door closed all in one motion and scraped the edges of the lock as she jammed the key into it. She pounded her fists on the steering wheel.

That infuriating old woman. She'd done everything she could think of to make Ellen like her. She sat politely at Sunday supper every week, gushing about the food, insisted on clearing the table and washing the dishes with a stupid old apron tied around her waist. Yes, she had tried hard to be the daughter Ellen MacBride wanted.

She knew from the beginning that Daniel was a mama's boy. Of course not in the clingy sense, but in the Irish-Catholic sense. He'd stand up for her to a point, but he must never be forced to choose, because Jennifer knew that she would lose.

She closed her eyes and took a deep breath. "I can't get upset, I can't get upset, I have to stay calm, have to keep my blood pressure down." She blew the breath out slowly.

Jennifer had noticed the boy with curly dark hair and warm brown eyes in the fourth grade. By the eighth grade, she had decided he was "the one". When her braces came off and her chest popped out, she worked hard to become a cheerleader. He played football and, as a cheerleader on the sidelines at every game, she would be impossible to ignore, right? Wrong, he ignored her!

And it was all because of that dorky Melissa Sullivan, the odd girl who lived in that mausoleum with weird old Mimi

Witherspoon. Melissa and Daniel were inseparable. Jennifer didn't know Melissa at all but she hated her anyway.

And worst of all, Ellen MacBride thought Melissa Sullivan hung the stars and the moon. But then, thank God, she had gone off to college and never come back. Off to New York to become a writer, or something, leaving Daniel pining away.

And leaving him to Jennifer, who waited and watched while he matured into the kind of man she needed. It took her almost two years to get him to go out but she had finally seduced him by telling him that she had saved herself all those years because she loved him. Now her patience had paid off and she had gotten the ring. A family would soon follow; sooner than Daniel knew. Everything was in place; it was all going to be fine. Jennifer was going to have everything she'd ever wanted.

She took another deep breath and turned the key.

As she drove past the front of the hospital, a woman with shoulder-length brown hair strode confidently through the automatic doors. Jennifer glanced her way, just as the sun caught the shine from the white streak over her right ear.

Jennifer slammed on the brakes and stared.

CHAPTER ELEVEN

After she left the hospital, Melissa dutifully returned to her aunts' house. She had forgotten how long a day could be in a quiet town.

She settled in a bit more, had lunch with Mimi and sparred with her almost amiably until her aunt needed a nap. Then she took a walk around town with Jane. The town was hanging on by exchanging the old hardware for an antiques shop, the little restaurant for an upscale coffee shop. There was a new mall about five miles up the road, Jane explained, with a Wal-Mart, a Home Depot, and a big box store. Everybody shopped there unless they needed something small right away. The town was drawing some trade from the university nearby; its professors and their wives thought it quaint. As long as the mill stayed open, Sylvan Mills would survive, she said with some pride.

When Melissa's cell phone yielded several more messages from her literary agent, the ever-nagging Barbara, she retired to her room to work on her second book so she could honestly say that progress was being made. She painfully pushed out a page or two before checking in on Ellen. She was pleased to hear that the doctors were impressed by the improvement in her condition.

She meandered into the kitchen and helped Jane fix a light dinner. Jane seemed distracted and was unusually quiet. Only when Melissa commented on the lovely scent wafting in from the garden did her face lighten. Even Mimi, who had insisted upon joining them at the table, kept glancing at her sister. But Jane kept her eyes lowered. When Melissa started clearing the table and Mimi was settled into the library with after-dinner coffee and a book,

Jane cleared her throat. Melissa looked at her at once, recognizing Jane's signal for serious discussion.

"Come with me a minute." Jane threw open the French doors in the dining room and waved Melissa through to the old rose garden, now a colorful, manicured vision. "Let me introduce you to the girls," she said with a flourish of one hand. She was rewarded by Melissa's gasp of appreciation.

Moving to the left, Jane tenderly cupped a small, perfect pink bloom. "This is Cecile. She's a polyanthus; full name Cecile Brunner. Pink, you know, is for gratitude and appreciation, so she likes attention." She went on to a fragrant, larger bloom of a deeper pink. "This is Louise. Her full name is Louise Odier, and she's a Bourbon, very big with the Victorians. Just smell that perfume!" She sniffed and stroked the rose gently before moving on. There was Sally Holmes and a Zeffie (Zephirine Drouhin) and more names than Melissa could remember.

It tickled Melissa's writer's mind to notice that it was Jane who was "blossoming" as she moved confidently amongst the antique roses. She knew their names, their histories, and their needs. Restoring the old garden was clearly a labor of love.

Finally, they came back to the doors and the last rosebush. "Now, the gallicas, albas, chinas, and damasks are all very old roses but here is my favorite: Rosa. She is very important and is believed to have been the red rose of the Lancasters in the War of the Roses. Rosa gallica officinalis. Isn't she magnificent?" She sighed appreciatively.

Melissa laughed out loud. "My lord, Aunt Jane, you've made quite a presentation here. You should be giving tours."

The woman blushed. "I do go on, I know. I joined the Garden Club, mostly, I suppose, so I could show off now and then."

Melissa bent down and hugged her aunt. "Nothin' wrong with that."

Jane squared her shoulders and her tone changed. "Thanks, sweetie. Now I'd like to ask you something."

"Sure, anything."

"This Witherspoon power that you have ... have you used it much ... since you left?"

Melissa shrugged. "Probably more than Mimi would approve of, that's for sure. I'd say a dozen times."

Jane nodded thoughtfully. "Does it ... hurt?"

"Yep. But it's worth it." She said lightly. "Let me give you an example. The first time was in college when my roommate, Patty, jumped to pull off a header on the soccer field. Somehow she came down on another player's foot and fell, her head actually bounced off the ground. I was the first one there." She shook her head.

"I forgot everything I'd been told about protection and stuff. I put both hands on her head and bam. The pain flew into my head so fast and hard that I guess I passed out and fell on top of her. When I came to, we were both at the hospital and she had a concussion and they thought I had simply fainted from the shock. But I know she'd had a fractured skull." She looked at her aunt. "I had made a difference; maybe saved her life. It was amazing to know that I had done that."

She continued. "But I had also learned my lesson about protecting myself. In my senior year, one of our housemates, Joanna, had been studying for a pre-med final for weeks and woke up with a cold or flu or something like that, sneezing and coughing, she was miserable. I, uh, pretended to feel her forehead for fever and quickly did the thing, you know. She took off down the stairs, thinking her cold relief medicine had really kicked in. I, on the other hand, took some of her cold medicine and went back to bed until my head stopped aching and my sinuses cleared."

Jane chuckled appreciatively. "That was good of you. "

"So now tell me what's brought on this interest all of a sudden."

Jane launched into what was clearly a prepared speech. "The reason I've been showing off my roses to you is to make you realize that people, like roses, are what they are because of the way they're treated. These roses were diseased, dying, and strangled in weeds a few years ago. They did the best they could, given the circumstances, just to survive. People do the same.

"There are a lot of things you don't know about Mimi. But if you could, just try to understand and accept that there are some things that would surely make you feel more ... compassionate toward her than you do. But I do understand how you feel, honey, I do."

Melissa was becoming more uncomfortable by the minute.

Seeing Melissa's face change, Jane hurried on. "Hear me out." She took a deep breath. "I asked you to come home because I knew she'd want to see you before she ... before anything happens to her and that she'd never call you herself. That's just the way it is.

"I was also hoping ... I'm not asking you to try to save her but she's in a lot of pain and it's going to get worse. So I wanted to know if it would really hurt you to help her. She's too proud to ask, but if you could ease things up a bit, toward the end, it would mean a lot to me.

"You're going to have to make your own decision. You're the one who's going to have to live with it. That's all I wanted to say." As soon as the last words were out of her mouth, her aunt quickly turned and went inside. Melissa found herself standing alone among the heady fragrance of the roses.

When she could move, she raced to her room and threw herself down on the bed. Chills ran down her spine. Help Mimi? Actually touch her? *Dear Jesus.* She had to talk to Stephen. The thought stopped her cold. She was so stupid.

He would have known that something like this would happen. It seemed pretty obvious now. Why wouldn't Jane expect her to do what she could to ease Mimi's passing? She wrapped both arms around the pillow. Mimi was the one who had explained it to her, passed on the ability, so to speak. It might have been the most words they ever exchanged ...

They had been sitting down to dinner and Melissa felt like crap. Aunt Jane had found her sobbing on her bed, convinced she was bleeding to death, and gently explained about menstrual cycles and helping her with the necessary products. Melissa had heard other girls at school talk about "getting their period" or "having their monthly" but never understood that it had anything to do with her. Jane gave her some pain relievers and showed her how to take care of herself. It was gross. She was feeling strange and out of sorts when she took her place at the dinner table. Absences were not excused.

The meal was eaten in the usual silence, although she felt Mimi's gaze on her. After dinner, when Aunt Jane had gone to the kitchen and Melissa stood up to go to her room, Mimi waved her back to her chair. She landed on the seat with a loud sigh. She just wanted to curl up in a ball on her bed.

"Sit, girl, sit. This won't take long. Let me see your hand." She had taken Melissa's left hand, palm up, and peered at it. Then she sighed. "Well, you have it, that's for sure."

Melissa looked at her own hand. She had what? What did she have besides a birthmark?

"Pay attention, Melissa. I do not like to repeat myself."

Melissa was fascinated. It was the first time she had ever seen the woman discomfited in any way.

"The women in our family, the Witherspoons that is, used to have ... a talent for helping people. You have no doubt read in the Bible about the laying on of hands?"

Melissa nodded. "Jesus was able to cure people of all kinds of illnesses by touching them."

Mimi looked relieved. "Exactly. It wasn't just Jesus, however. If you research more closely, you will find that some of the disciples had this ability as well. It is a longstanding tradition in many faiths. How some of this ability came to our family, I have no idea. I'm sure you have also studied the witch trials in school?"

"Sure. They took place in Salem, mostly. Lots of innocent women accused of being witches were drowned and burned and stuff. It was pretty much a lie."

"Correct. However, many of the women accused of being witches were actually healers and did have certain abilities. They used herbs and folk medicine and, occasionally, the laying on of hands to help people. Because they were different, they were feared and sometimes persecuted."

Melissa's felt anxious. "You're not saying we're witches?"

Mimi looked shocked. "Of course not. We never were witches in the black cat, broomstick, evil sense. Lord, no. If there was some, shall we say, white witch capacity among us, those days are past. Our grandmothers may have had such skills but, you see, they seem to have faded with each generation. Now, considering your situation, you must be careful how and when you decide to utilize these ... skills. First of all, it can be very draining on you physically. I believe that every healing you do takes a little something out of you forever."

She shrugged and continued. "Others may disagree. But it definitely weakens you to absorb other people's pain. Secondly and most importantly, Melissa, it can be unwise to tell just anyone. People do fear that which they do not understand. At the least, it can make them uncomfortable. Simply put, your friends and later on, your boyfriends especially, may turn and run." Her face hardened. "However, it is possible, if used infrequently and discreetly, to live with it. Am I clear?"

"Not really."

"Very well." She sighed. "I see I must teach by example. You are in some distress right now. Women troubles. Am I right?"

"Yes ma'am." Melissa blushed.

"Well, I am going to use my ... ability to ease your pain. Close your eyes."

Melissa did as she was told. She felt Mimi's long bony hand press against her stomach through her jeans and tried not to cringe. Within a minute or two, the cramps faded.

"You may open your eyes." Melissa did and saw that Mimi looked a bit pale. "Well, as you can tell, I was able to withdraw some of your pain. It was a small thing." She managed a tight-lipped smile. "Unfortunately, you cannot do this for yourself, that's one of the drawbacks to the gift."

"How did you do that?" Melissa asked. "Could my mother do it? How come she never told me about this? Can Aunt Jane do it?"

Her aunt raised a long hand to stop the barrage of questions. "First things first, let me show you how to protect yourself."

She had gone on to instruct Melissa, told her bluntly that neither Jane nor Emily had the ability as there was typically one such "talent" per generation in the immediate family, and then retreated as soon as possible to her room, her duty completed.

They hadn't discussed it since. Melissa had found her own way, finding a hard-won comfort with her gift. She had to admit that Mimi had been right about a thing or two. Using it was easier than explaining it and it had cost her every relationship with a man she'd ever truly cared about, until Stephen. *Maybe.*

She punched in his number on her cell phone and waited. Suddenly his voice came through the line. "Stephen Callahan."

When she realized he hadn't looked at the number, she hurried on. "It's me. I know you're upset. I'm sorry, Stephen. I couldn't tell you in person that I was leaving. I knew you would have tried to talk me out of it and I needed to come right away. I'm sorry."

She heard him sigh and pictured him sitting at his desk, shoving back his sandy hair with one hand as it fell across his forehead, and then pushing his glasses up on his nose.

She hurried on. "I came because Jane called me, you know that. Mimi is dying."

He hesitated just a moment. "What is it?"

"Cancer, metastasized, in the final stages. The doctors say there's nothing to do but try to keep her comfortable and control the pain as much as possible. That's another reason why I called. I need to talk to you about something." She gulped. "Jane's asked me to help her. I ... don't know if I can do it."

She listened to the thoughtful silence, then the thoughtful question. "You can't or you won't? Which is it, Melissa?"

"I'm not sure. I don't know. I hate being put in this position. Do you realize that the woman has never touched me except to show me how, you know, to do the thing? She never once hugged me or patted my head or ..." Melissa felt herself choking up. "I know Jane means well, but she doesn't realize ..."

"I would imagine she realizes more than anyone else, Mel." His voice was firm.

"What should I do?" she blurted out.

He was silent for a few seconds then he chuckled. "This isn't the most analytical or professional answer I've ever given anyone, but I have to suggest that you sleep on it. You don't have to decide today, do you?"

"Not really, I guess." She felt relief flowing through her.

"Okay, so why don't you sit with it for a day or so and see how it feels? Your initial reaction may or may not be the one that's best for either of you."

She paused. "I guess I could call Magee. She's probably wondering how things are going. I talked to her before I left New York."

"You spoke to Magee before you left?" He didn't need to say anything more because they both heard the rest of the sentence. He decided to let it go.

"She knows about my strained relationship with Mimi and said it might be good for both of us if we could make peace before ..."

She paused, then hurried on. "Let's talk about something else."

He hesitated for only a second or two. "I can do that. Mom called for you."

"Oh, I'm sorry I missed her. Is everything okay? Did you tell her I was out of town?"

"Everything's fine. She wanted to ask if you would help her plan a birthday party for Dad's sixtieth. She wants to have a dinner somewhere, maybe invite some of his army buddies, that kind of thing. I told her you had to go out of town for a couple of days."

"You didn't tell her where I am, did you?" She wasn't sure why it mattered but it seemed to at the moment.

"She thinks it's about the new book and I didn't go into details."

Melissa loved Stephen's loud, happy family, and how they loved parties! Any birthday, anniversary or graduation was cause for a big celebration. Stephen's sister and one brother were comfortably married and settled down; his other brother was a priest, which made Stephen and Melissa the brunt of much teasing and speculation at family gatherings.

"You know I'd love to help, but she and Shannon will probably have everything in order by the time I get back. But I'll be there."

His voice went quieter. "Will you, Melissa?"

"Of course, I wouldn't miss your dad's birthday. I just don't know how long I'll be here. It could be a couple of days or a couple of weeks. I'm sorry to be so vague, but it's hard to know." Silence at the other end. "Well, I better let you go, but I'll call again soon."

"I love you, Mel, and I miss you."

"Love you, too." She answered without thinking. After she hung up, she started to relax, felt her shoulders lower as the tension ebbed.

She could wait, think it over, and see what happened.

CHAPTER TWELVE

The rest of Daniel's day had gone very differently but was just as upsetting. After he sat in his office for an hour, thinking about the impact of Melissa's return on the town, the one person he was most concerned about was Sally Walters. It had been far too easy for her to blurt out the secret of Melissa's parentage to him.

Jerry at the local bar had called him, as he often did, to pick her up. As his jeep pulled up to the curb, she staggered out of the bar. When he stopped with a squeal of brakes and jumped out, she giggled and grabbed his arm.

"Sally." He made his voice stern. "Come on, I'll take you home."

She smiled lazily. "Gotta go home. Good girl. Gotta go home."

"That's right." He helped her into the Jeep and struggled to buckle her seat belt which amused her greatly.

"Now, Danny, you watch those hands. I may like a little fun, but I'm in a whatchamacallit, 'committed relationship,' these days."

He slammed the door. "Glad to hear it." He walked around and slid in behind the wheel.

"You betcha. 'Bout time good ol' Sally gets a break. We're talking the man of my dreams, darlin'. Easy street. Good times." She reached into her purse and pulled out a pack of cigarettes.

"No smoking in the vehicle."

"No problem." She opened the window and lit up, took a puff, blew the smoke out the window in perfect circles, and dangled her arm out over the window, cigarette and all.

Daniel sighed.

She laid her head back against the headrest and closed her eyes as he headed toward the trailer outside of town where she lived with her alcoholic father.

After a few minutes, she spoke again. "So you're finally gonna make an honest woman out of Jennifer, huh?"

"Looks like it."

She looked at him and smiled. "Well, she's done her time waitin', I guess. You do carry a torch, gotta give you that."

Frown lines deepened around his eyes and mouth.

"Oh, don't get your shorts in a twist, Danny. But that girl was trouble from the day she was born." Her eyes crinkled. "That was a good one."

"What the hell are you talking about?" he asked gruffly.

She snickered. "Shhhh, it's a big secret. Thanks to my new connections over at the courthouse, I found out some pretty interesting stuff about your darling little Melissa, baby." She lowered her voice to what she apparently thought was a whisper. "You'll never guess who her real parents are!"

"Her parents are—were—Rob and Emily Sullivan, Sally, you know that."

She shook her head and stopped when it made her dizzy. She pulled in her cigarette, took a puff, and blew the smoke out the window. "Nah-uh. So I know something you don't know," she said in a childish sing-song voice. Then she told him.

After a rough and rocking ride up the lane, the Jeep came to a peaceful halt in front of the forlorn Walters trailer. Daniel composed himself, his brain racing.

"Listen, Sal, you have to keep quiet about this. Whether this is true or not, and it sure doesn't seem likely, God only knows what would happen if they find out you're talking this around, you hear me?"

She sulked. "I'm only telling you. If I can't trust you, Danny, who can I trust?"

He helped her out of the car and walked her to the door, holding on to her arm and giving her another warning.

"Remember, nothing about this to anybody. It's really important, Sally. Are you listening to me?"

She nodded unhappily, and blew him a kiss before disappearing inside.

Ever since that night, he'd been trying to come up with a course of action. Paramount, of course, was making sure Sally kept this to herself for her own safety. Then there was the question of whether Daniel should tell and whom?

He considered telling Melissa. Everyone deserved to know where they came from and who they were. God, when her book came out, ironically titled *Who Am I*, it nearly killed him. But it also made him realize how fragile her mental stability was and he was not going to be the one to push her over the edge. Call it rationalizing, but he couldn't do it.

It was tempting to call up her father. He absolutely deserved to have his disavowal and neglect of his illegitimate daughter see the light of day. It would be the end of his political climb to the governor's mansion, that's for sure.

It would be a pleasure to call her mother and knock her down a few pegs. The whole town would enjoy that.

At the end of the day, he decided to let sleeping dogs lie. These were powerful people, the heavyweights in this town, and one or both would go out of their way to destroy Sally and she had so little as it was. He didn't deny that they would come after him as well. It didn't feel like the bravest thing he'd ever done.

Not telling Melissa was the hardest part.

Now she was back, and unless she had changed considerably, how long would it take her to stir up a hornet's nest? Despite his warnings, Sally had a mouth on her, and if she ran into Melissa, could she resist the urge to play "I know something you don't know," as she had with him?

He called Sally's cell and left a message for her to call him. Then he spent a few hours completing the registration forms for the training course his three rookies were going to take at Penn State, finished off some other routine paperwork, and helped out at a standoff between an irate farmer with a shotgun and his neighbor. She returned his call just as he was calling it quits for the day.

"Hey, good lookin. What's up?"

"Sally, Melissa Sullivan's back in town."

She giggled. "Thanks for the news flash, Danny. But that's old news. Everybody knows that."

Of course they did. He sighed. "Listen kiddo. Remember that conversation we had that concerned Melissa? It's more important now that she's here."

She was quiet for a moment. "Right. I get it. My lips are sealed. No problem."

"Good girl. You be careful, okay? And if you run into any trouble, you call me right away."

"Thanks." She answered soberly. "I mean it. You're a good man." Then she giggled again. "But you worry too much." Then she hung up.

Daniel didn't know what more he could do so he headed over to Jennifer's house. She wanted to talk.

CHAPTER THIRTEEN

Brian Jackson was standing at his window, lost in thought, when she pulled into the lot. The red car caught his eye. He couldn't believe it; he'd told Sally quite specifically never to come here.

She burst into his office and the look on his face didn't stop her from telling him the news. Thank God every attorney had to be a good actor. He let her go on for about half an hour, nodding at appropriate intervals, about how they'd better set the date, sooner rather than later.

From the same window, he watched her leave. She looked up into the setting sun and waved. He smiled and waved back.

Just that morning, Garrett Anniston had warned him when he corralled him in the men's room. The man had let him know what was what in a few sentences ...

"Sally Walters."

Brian's eyes widened.

The smile tightened. "Yes, I know you've been discreet. There's very little that goes on in this county that I don't know about. It would behoove you to remember that."

"Yes, sir."

Anniston responded to the puzzled expression on the younger man's face. "Let me extend you the courtesy of being direct here, Brian. The girl's a slut; has been since she was about thirteen, and has a big mouth to boot. So, when I hear rumors that a potentially important young man, especially one of my ADAs, is getting involved with her, I feel duty-bound to speak up."

Brian had felt his face going from white to red. Now it felt very pale again.

He was lucky to get this job. It hadn't been easy from the beginning. His grades at Penn didn't exactly bring the offers pouring in. Then at his last job, his only other job, there was a scandal. It wasn't his fault but it was way too easy to dump it on him and save the reputation of a partner. His father had made a few calls, one to Garrett Anniston, and now he was killing time in this burg, trying to earn his way back to civilization. Sally ... she was so sweet, so naïve in a small town way. Brian sighed. He was going to miss her.

After she pulled out of the lot, he picked up the phone and dialed the number. Within an hour, he was sitting in the library of one of the largest houses in town.

"So, Brian, you've a bigger problem than we thought."

Brian cleared his throat. "I'm sure it's not unmanageable, sir. We ... I'll just give her money to leave town and have the kid somewhere else."

Garrett sighed, walked from behind his desk, set his drink on a coaster atop an antique table, and sat down in the matching high-backed brown leather chair opposite to the one Brian occupied. "Son, are you aware that Sally has a father here?"

"Sure, she's mentioned him."

"Has she ever, in the course of your ... relationship, not gone home to her father? You know, stayed overnight with you?"

Brian's voice was almost unintelligible. "No."

It was Garrett's turn to nod. "And she won't, either. He an alcoholic and she's been taking care of him her whole life. She'll never leave this town, Brian." He let the silence build.

At the stern tone of his voice, Brian felt beads of sweat pop out on his forehead. "Maybe she'll get an abortion if I ask her to ..."

In a sad tone, Garrett replied, "It's as if you don't know this girl at all, Brian. That is not going to be an option. If you ask her to get an abortion, it will be all over town before the words are out of your mouth."

"So what do you suggest?" He tried to sound mature and businesslike.

The look on Garrett's face said he was thinking deeply. "Well, let me see what I can do. You do nothing for now. You'll hear something within 24 hours." He stood and walked to the library door and pulled it open, indicating that the short meeting was over.

As Brian walked past him, relief showed on his face. "Thanks, Garrett. I really appreciate it."

Anniston's eyes were cold. "Yes, I expect you will."

After the front door closed, Garrett settled into his comfortable armchair and finished his drink with a smile on his face. This was working out well for him, as things usually did. It was too bad about Sally, it really was. Surely she never expected to grow old anyway, living the way she did. It had been a stroke of genius, he admitted to himself modestly, to approach Brian. His face hardened. The boy deserved to be party to the solution since it appeared to Garrett that he had helped to create the problem.

Rumors had been passed to him that Sally knew about Melissa's parentage. That would simply not do. He had issued a quiet reminder through the grapevine of the courthouse that silence was golden but talking out of turn might prove to be detrimental to one's employment, health and happiness.

In the meantime, Sally was a loose cannon. Even if he had a private chat with her, he wasn't sure it was genetically possible for her to keep her mouth shut long term.

He could scarcely have hoped that Brian would have come around so soon. Now that Sally was pregnant and a problem, he believed that Garrett was doing him a favor. The guy was still wet behind the ears and had no idea the power he was handing Garrett. Now he would be on board for the upcoming elections and in his debt forever. Garrett liked to have his people in line.

He picked up his cell phone and hit a speed dial number. "I will need your help after all. Yes. Thank you."

He went upstairs to read some business correspondence and dictate some letters for his secretary for the morning. Then, as always, he read a few chapters of his Bible before turning in.

CHAPTER FOURTEEN

Melissa went to the hospital first thing in the morning and found Ellen propped up against her pillows, reading "Who Am I?"

She smiled at Melissa and pointed at the book. "I've a few questions for ya."

"Okay. I'll answer three questions and then you have to put that thing away. Deal?"

Ellen nodded. "Ya tried ta commit suicide and ware in a mental hospital?"

"That's not a question. It's a fact," Melissa answered calmly. She'd been through this many times. She absently twisted the white streak in her hair around her fingers.

"Ya cut off ya're hair with a knife?" Ellen was watching her as she spoke.

"I guess I couldn't find any scissors. Stephen says it was rejection of the Witherspoons, particularly Mimi." She grinned. "Go figure."

"Stephen?"

"Stephen is a psychologist and my boyfriend, not my therapist, a fact he's prone to forget, which can be pretty annoying, but occasionally useful."

"Okay." Ellen took several short breaths. "Back ta the mental hospital, then. Tell me 'bout it."

"It's not as bad as you think." Melissa's words sounded defensive even to herself and she shrugged. "It's worse."

"So, in the little notes ya sent along ta me, why is it ya ne'er mentioned anya this?" She looked at Melissa sternly over her bifocals.

"There was nothing you could have done and I didn't want to upset you." Melissa hesitated and laid a warm hand on Ellen's. "Now that's three questions and then some. You shouldn't be thinking about this right now. I'm fine. Remember, this is a novel." She traced the black letters on the silver book cover. "The first four times I wrote the ending, Amanda committed suicide." She shrugged. "Happy endings sell better so my editor made me keep trying. I wrote it under my own name just to embarrass Mimi." Her smile widened and she raised her eyebrows.

"And Adam an' Amanda?" Ellen watched Melissa's face carefully.

Melissa's face went still but she kept her tone mild. "Ah, can't wait for the sequel, huh? To tell you the truth, I haven't gotten too far on it but don't tell my publisher." She looked down at the bed. "I can tell you, though, that in the sequel Amanda has gotten stronger, which threatens Adam's rescue fantasy. There are some lovely dramatic confrontations, however. And not to worry, we are monitoring the situation with great interest. Now you've got the inside scoop and let's talk about something else."

She was suddenly aware of someone standing in the doorway behind her. Melissa turned to look, automatically tucking the white streak of hair behind her right ear. "Hello, Daniel."

She felt incredibly stupid, like the pounding in her chest was drowning out the signals from her brain. Yes, he looked exactly as she had imagined he would—the broad shoulders of a big man but with the same soft, curly dark hair and the same warm-brown eyes of the boy. He was different, though. It might have been the frown lines that he was too young to have, or the way he was looking at her. There was no welcome in his face.

"Melissa. Thanks for coming. I know Ma appreciates it." There was no welcome in his voice, either.

Not exactly the reunion Melissa had dreamed of over the years but she refused to make an ass of herself. She swallowed her disappointment, willed her heart to slow down, and matched his cool tone. "Of course, I'm so glad to see her, too."

In the silence that followed, she discarded a dozen clever and casual remarks. She was sure Daniel watched them flicker across her face and was content to wait. Ultimately, she decided escape seemed the best route, not brilliant but effective.

She glanced down at her watch. "Gosh, look at the time. I better go pay some attention to the aunts."

Ellen, seeing her discomfort, said nothing as Melissa leaned down and kissed her cheek. "Bye for now, but I'll see you soon." She squeezed her hand.

Melissa gave Daniel a curt nod as she cut a wide swatch around him and swept from the room. If cool was what he wanted, frozen is what he'd get. She'd be Melissa Sullivan, ice queen.

Daniel sank into the chair Melissa had vacated, trying not to think about how she looked and how she sounded and the fact that the chair was still warm. Ellen reached over and ruffled his curls.

He pulled away and his hand fell with a slap on the book she had slid under the top sheet. "Ma, you need to concentrate on getting better, not on this crap."

"Don't be tellin' me what I can and canna do, young man," Ellen answered firmly. "I wanted ta know. And I wanted ta see 'er face when she told me."

Frustration at seeing Melissa sparked the simmering anger left from last night's unresolved argument with Jennifer to full burn. Daniel exploded bitterly, "She shouldn't have come here, Ma. She'll just upset everybody, and then take off again and we'll all be left picking up the pieces."

"Now wouldn't that be soundin' like Jennifer, or her mother, talkin'?" she retorted without hesitation.

Daniel glared at her; she returned his look evenly. He stalked out.

Ellen lay there, thinking. So they hadn't fallen into each other's arms. That was nothing but the stubborn in both of them. A small bit a pride, she thought to herself. Melissa was home and her beloved children were going to work this out, once and for all. It was meant to be. A smile touched the corners of Ellen's mouth as she dozed off.

Daniel caught up to Melissa in the lobby. "Melissa."

Her fading color started to return as she raised those damned tawny eyes to his. "I'd appreciate it if you'd remember my mother is not well. This is not a good time to get her upset about your ... problems." Daniel fixed her with his best police chief glare. It helped him focus.

She nodded. "I was just thinking the same thing. I've got to do better at deflecting her questions and keeping it upbeat."

Her agreeable response caught him off guard. The confusion flashed across his face and Melissa couldn't keep from reacting. Her face lightened into the smile that used to stop his heart.

"Okay." He replied gruffly and strode away.

Melissa walked to the parking lot, muttering to herself. "Welcome home, Melissa. How have you been? It's nice to see you. Nice to see you too, Daniel. Miss me?"

CHAPTER FIFTEEN

Ellen asked her to go. So later that afternoon, Melissa turned the knob and, of course, the front door was unlocked, as it always had been. Ellen's house was exactly as Melissa remembered it: white lace curtains, Victorian hurricane lamps with roses on the bowls and shades, a dark carved banister ideal for sliding down. She moved from room to room, running her fingers over the furniture, feeling for the scratches she knew would be there.

She heard pounding over the hardwood floors and a big old golden retriever came barreling from the back of the house towards her.

"Lily!" She exclaimed.

Upon hearing her name, the old dog jumped up on Melissa and knocked her off balance. She went down to her knees and threw her arms around the thick neck. "I can't believe it's you."

The dog licked her face frantically and Melissa laughed despite the tears that seemed to suddenly appear in her eyes. How long had it been? She remembered vividly the day they found Lily. It had to be over thirteen years ago because she was thirteen and Daniel was fifteen. She kept her arms around the dog while the memories flooded through her.

Daniel and Melissa walked home from school, hand in hand, their books tucked under Daniel's left arm. A golden retriever followed at a safe distance, her flag tail waving hopefully.

Melissa kept looking back at her. "Daniel, wait a minute. Come here, girl." Melissa bent down.

The dog hesitated. Cautious brown eyes stayed on Daniel as the animal came forward to her outstretched hand. Melissa petted her smooth broad head. "Isn't she beautiful, Daniel?"

He looked skeptically down at the big dog. "She probably belongs to someone, Missy. She don't look like she's starvin'."

"Doesn't. And she doesn't have a collar or tags."

"That *doesn't* mean anything around here, half the dogs in town don't. Come on, Missy. Let her go. We're late."

"'Bye, girl." She gave the dog a final pet and looked back over her shoulder as Daniel grabbed her hand and pulled her on down the street.

The next day, she kept an eye out for the dog but it was nowhere to be seen. It wasn't as if Aunt Mimi would ever let her have a pet anyway. When Melissa had put out a timid feeler on the subject, she had made it perfectly clear that animals meant "hair all over everything, eating the food right off the table, dirty, disgusting creatures, licking and scratching, and the very thought makes me ill."

Another week passed before the dog appeared behind them again. Melissa petted her, giving Daniel a pleading look, but he shook his head. "You know your aunt will never let you keep her."

Melissa set her jaw. "I'm going to ask."

Daniel shrugged. "You're just gonna get yelled at."

She coaxed the dog home, Daniel following behind. She marched up the steps and into the house, the dog at her side. Daniel sat down on the wall at the edge of the yard and waited.

"Aunt Mimi? Aunt Jane?"

"Hi, sweetie." Jane came out of the kitchen and saw the dog. "Oh, my!"

Melissa looked at her pleadingly. "Can I keep her? Please, Aunt Jane? Isn't she beautiful?"

"Oh, honey, you know how Mimi feels about animals in the house." She stroked the broad head absently. "She'll just pitch a fit, Melissa." She sighed. "I'm sorry, honey."

Mimi came in from the garden, looking at her watch. She stopped dead at the sight of the dog, her sister, and Melissa in the hall. Her voice boomed across the room. "What is that?"

Melissa spun. "Please, Aunt Mimi, can I keep her? She followed me home from school. Please?"

Mimi Witherspoon straightened to her full five feet, ten inches, her thin spine stiff, her eyes frigid. "Melissa, I believe I have made my feelings on this subject perfectly clear."

Melissa's eyes filled. "Please. I can take care of her. She won't be any trouble."

"There will be no further discussion. Remove that thing from my home. You will not bring the matter up again. And I will be speaking with you after dinner about this behavior, Melissa."

Melissa took the dog outside. Daniel slid down off the stone wall and swiped at the back of his pants.

"I told you. You shouldn't have tried. She's gonna ground you just for asking, right?" He was annoyed. "What about the band?"

She started to cry again.

"You never learn, Missy."

Back at his house, Daniel and Melissa sat on the porch swing, planning the next day. He had football practice after school; she had chess club. But, in the evenings, he usually played guitar while she sang; Daniel was trying to put together a band to pick up some extra money. Now it was a question of just how long Melissa would be grounded.

Daniel disappeared inside and she sat there, trying to ignore the brown eyes looking trustingly at her from beside her feet. The door swung open and Ellen MacBride dried her hands on her apron and sat down on the swing next to

Melissa. Daniel leaned against the doorframe, watching his mother.

She looked at the dog, her son, and then at Melissa. "Well, I'll not be the one feedin' it and walkin' it twice a day, I'm tellin' ya that right now."

"Oh!" A smile lit up her pale face and Melissa threw her arms around Ellen's neck. "Mrs. MacBride, you're the best. You're just the best. I have enough money saved to pay for a vet if she needs one. Thank you, thank you."

The little woman patted her arms, disentangled herself, and went back into the house, shaking her head.

"Thank you, Daniel, thank you."

He tried to look tough but changed his mind as Melissa's warm arms wrapped around his neck.

They scrounged up some old metal bowls for the dog and laid some blankets down.

"Whatcha gonna call her?" Daniel asked, petting the muzzle lying across his knee.

Melissa said, "I have to give it some thought. I'll tell you tomorrow." He and the dog walked her home.

Warmth spread through her. Despite everything, despite Mimi, she really couldn't remember ever being happier than she was then. She sat there on the floor with a contented smile, petting the soft fur. Then she heard footsteps coming up the front porch.

CHAPTER SIXTEEN

Daniel pushed the front door open, and then stared at her and the dog on the floor of his entry hall.

She hastily wiped her face with her hands and said, "Ellen asked me to walk the dog. She thought you might be too busy."

He shook his head. "She never gives up." The dog broke loose and ran over to lick Daniel's hand. He rubbed her head reflexively. "It's still a stupid name for a dog."

Lily spotted the open door behind him and ran for it. Daniel reached down to grab her by the collar, as Melissa rushed over and pushed it shut. Lily jerked Daniel towards the door as Melissa turned, pinning her against it.

They were touching each other for the first time since she had come back and it was full body contact. Their heartbeats echoed each other's, and they felt each other's breath. Melissa was afraid to move or speak. He slid his hand up the door to brace his weight and push himself away.

She raised her head to look him in the eye. "Daniel," she whispered hoarsely.

He blinked first. "Don't." He forced the word from a dry throat.

She kissed him softly anyway. Any restraint he might have had flew out the window as he responded to her mouth and her body.

"Oh, Christ," Daniel muttered as he picked her up and carried her up the stairs as if she were a child. The dog, forgotten now, lay down by the door, watching them reproachfully.

Daniel picked her up, placed her on the bed, and undressed her slowly, like a gift he wanted to savor. She was afraid to breathe for fear of breaking the spell. Her body trembled. He kissed her gently, then pulled away and moved down her body until he was kissing her toes. He worked his way up her thighs to her belly to her breasts to her neck. When he finally reached her lips, she parted them and his warm tongue slid inside. She thought she would explode without him going any farther. She grabbed him and tore his clothes off.

Although just minutes had passed, she moaned softly as his body covered hers. They fitted together like lock and key, just as she always knew they would.

Melissa sighed. That dreamy interlude, courtesy of every romance novel she'd ever read, complete with background music, was still only a dream. Their bodies had known what to do but she lost him somewhere along the way.

As soon as they had collapsed panting next to each other, Daniel had turned away, sat up on the edge of the bed and pulled on his clothes as fast as he could. Without even looking at her, he mumbled, "I have to walk the dog and get back to the station." The slam of the front door echoed through the empty house.

Melissa laid there in his bed in stupefied silence until she began to feel like a trespasser. She struggled into her own clothes and crept out.

He hadn't said, "I love you" or "I've always loved you, Melissa." He hadn't even said how glad he was she had come back. The only emotion she had glimpsed in his face as he ran away was—disappointment.

Back in her own room, it was all she could think about as she crumpled the pillow against her face. *Disappointment!* Accepting reality had never been her strong suit but she had never expected this. She had waited so long. Tears glistened in her eyes. It wasn't fair. She pounded her pillow into submission, well aware that she was acting like a six-year-old, a hurt and rejected six-year-old.

When she calmed down, she began to listen to the inner voice that seemed to be a side effect of the Witherspoon gift. It forced her to be honest with herself even when she didn't want to hear it. *Like now.* She remembered a boy and long dreamed about coming back to him; but she'd made love to a man who was a stranger to her. It was hot, it was exciting, and then it was over. Was that what Daniel had realized?

She heard Stephen's voice in her head, telling her one more time that she had built a fantasy around Sylvan Mills that couldn't possibly come true. *Damn you, Stephen. And damn you too, Daniel. And damn all men in general.*

Just before she fell asleep, she thought of a fitting title for her new book, the sequel to *Who Am I?* She could call it *What Am I Doing Here?*

CHAPTER SEVENTEEN

Sally was humming, tapping her nails on the steering wheel as she drove to the park and their special spot.

What would he do tonight? In the back of her mind, she was sure he would propose. Maybe roses and a beautiful ring. Her own diamond! She was glad the sneaking around would be over. In the beginning it made her feel sort of special, like she had a delicious secret no one else had. But now she wanted to be his wife, accepted and respected for all the world to see. She glanced at the clock on the radio, pushed her foot down on the accelerator, and smiled.

=======

He sat in the dark in the beat-up old Chevy. Sally Walters. He remembered her mother, Carol. Now there was a beauty. He missed her still but probably not half as much as the old man did. He sighed. At least she'd had the good sense to run--and keep going.

He saw her headlights in the distance and got out of the car. As he moved to the tree line, his heart began to beat faster. He didn't mind the money but he'd have done it for free; killing women didn't bother him much. He'd gotten over that in Nam. Women carried explosives, too, and more than a few of his buddies lost their asses to pretty little gooks. He was trained to be ruthless, feel nothing, and follow orders. The belt wrapped around both hands tightened involuntarily. He made absolutely no sound as he moved toward the benches. He had learned that in Nam, too.

=======

Brian was drunk. He sat in the study with a bottle of Jack and checked the time. A sudden flood of emotion made him catch his breath. It hit him that, when this was over, when Sally was gone, so was his child. His son? A little girl with his mother's eyes? He stumbled to his desk, grabbing for the phone, knocking it onto the floor. He dove at it and punched the numbers.

"C'mon...C'mon."

"Yes?"

"Oh God, you gotta stop this! I can't do this! Call it off. Please!"

"It's rather late, sir, and I believe you have the wrong number." Garrett said and replaced the receiver.

Brian sat back on his haunches and fell back against the bookcase as the phone went dead.

CHAPTER EIGHTEEN

Daniel had waited too long and his worst fears had come true. Yesterday was a blur after he left Melissa alone in his bed. Every instinct told him to find Sally, but he had not listened. He was willing to admit that a part of him refused to believe that someone in town would actually hurt her.

Now she was missing. One of his guys had filled out some half-assed report and thrown it on the file clerk's desk out front. Daniel just happened to be on his way in when he heard the guy chuckle and mention the Walters name. He had grabbed the paper and taken it with him into his office. He should have had it yesterday. Should have been doing his job yesterday instead of ...

Daniel was already feeling like a bone being fought over by two dogs, Jennifer and his mother, and his infidelity sat in his stomach like acid. The bitter office coffee wasn't going to help. He rubbed his eyes and leaned back in his chair.

Christ, he hoped she'd taken off for a few days with some trucker. Because if she hadn't, it meant the fallout he had feared was starting. Was Melissa's father capable of such a thing? He didn't want to know. Yet he couldn't convince himself that Sally had, coincidentally, disappeared right now. He had to find her; he had to at least look.

Jen was expecting him for lunch. He slid the report above the Jeep's sun visor and drove out of the station parking lot. He stopped at the Old Airport Road intersection and looked both ways. Five minutes to the right was lunch with Jennifer; ten minutes the other way was the Walters trailer where Sally lived with her dad. Daniel checked his watch and made the left turn. He regretted it almost immediately as the Jeep hit the rutted dirt and gravel. At least there was no one around to see the chief of police wincing in pain and muttering curses as the rock and roll caused his old football neck injury to flare up.

He came to a grateful halt in front of the old metal trailer that most passersby would have taken for abandoned. Thin weeds meandered half-heartedly up the corroded sheeting, the windows were filthy with road dust, and the front-end hookup was rusted off. Torn bags of trash and crumpled newspapers had long since replaced grass in the yard. At the back, a few shriveled tomato plants lay defeated and some faded towels hung on a sagging clothesline.

He grabbed the unsigned report. I wouldn't have signed it either, he thought, as he tucked it into his shirt pocket and made his way toward the door. Daniel knocked solidly on the thin metal and a family of spiders ran for their lives. The worn latch fell open and he ducked inside. The interior of the trailer showed the same degree of care as the exterior but smelled worse, the unwashed sour smell of a longtime drinker.

"Hey, Johnny. It's Dan MacBride. You here?"

He picked his way to the back room, over empty beer bottles and crumpled newspapers, following the sounds of snorts and grunts. Johnny Walters lay sprawled sideways across a bed with dirty sheets tangled around him. Daniel picked up the bony old man and turned his head against the smell of sweat, liquor, and urine. He carried him carefully to the couch, cleared a space with a sweep of his arm, and propped him up in the corner.

"John, it's Dan MacBride. I came to talk to you about Sally." The old man squinted at him. "Come on, man, shake it off and talk to me. Where's Sally?"

"I ain't deaf, you know." The deep voice was raspy from infrequent conversation and frequent tobacco. "She ain't here. That's the point, ain't it? Somethin' bad's happened to her. I told 'em, somethin' bad. They don't give a shit about me an' my girl. Ain't as good as some 'round here, I guess." He wiped his nose with the back of his hand.

Daniel rubbed a hand across his forehead, trying to loosen the tension headache. "So you think Sally's missing and came in to report it, John?"

"Sure did. My girl's gone, ain't she? I got rights, ain't I? Went right in and got throwed out on my ear. That guinea sonofabitch laughed in my face." He glared at Daniel. "My girl's been gone since yesterday. She don't stay out all night, never has."

Daniel swallowed and counted to ten. "Okay, okay. I understand you're upset. But I'm here and I'm trying to help. If I'm going to find her, I need to ask you some questions. You up to it?"

"Gimme a minute." The old man shuffled down the hall to the bathroom and came back with damp face and hair. "Okay. Shoot. Won't do no good, but you kin ask, makes ya feel better."

"Why would you say that? Have you heard from her?"

Johnny shook his head. "She's dead. Mus' be or I'd a heard from 'er." He sniffled, felt his pocket for a tobacco can that wasn't there and sighed. "All 'ere is to it. Ain't comin' back."

Daniel sighed in turn. "Let's hope for the best until we know different. Okay? Last time you saw her?"

"She went out 'round noon, I'm a thinkin'."

"And she didn't come back?"

"Not that I knows of." He shuffled uncomfortably. "I's sleepin' in the back most o' the day." He paused then insisted stubbornly. "If she coulda, she'd a come home by now."

"You didn't hear anybody come in, a fight, screams, anything like that?" Daniel asked hopefully.

"Nope."

"Was she mad at you? Were you two fighting?" He figured he might as well cover all the bases.

"No more 'n usual." The old man sniffed, started pawing the sofa for his snuff can.

"She wasn't thinking of going anywhere?"

"She weren't talkin' 'bout leavin' town if that's what ya mean." He hesitated. "I ain't been thinkin' 'bout nothin' else, chief. She didn't have no one come 'round here, mostly met 'em in town. I ain't around that much myself." He stared at the floor.

Or conscious that much, Daniel thought. He stood to ease the cramp in his legs and a black kitten came out from under the sofa and brushed against his ankle, purring. He bent down and picked it up. "Okay, John. Let me check this out." He made his voice stern and authoritative. "You have to understand that she's only been gone 24 hours at most. Just because she's never stayed out before doesn't mean she didn't last night. You've got to hold it together in case she calls or tries to contact you. Here's my cell number. Okay?" He put the kitten down and handed him a card.

Johnny stood up and put the card in his shirt pocket, concentrating on his ramrod straight posture, shaking just a little. "Okay, chief." He put a snuff-stained hand out and Daniel shook it firmly. "You're a good man, jus' like your daddy was."

Daniel nodded, unable to think of an answer to that. The old man was right; it was not like Sally to leave him alone with no word. For whatever he was and wasn't, he was still her father. That "guinea sonofabitch" had to be Lou Vinterra, his personal cross to bear. The dust cloud surrounding his Jeep reflected his frame of mind as he bounced back down the road, "A good man like my Daddy was."

CHAPTER NINETEEN

Daniel's father, Thomas MacBride, was indeed a good man, and none to say different. His family was descended from those who had first come to work in the Witherspoon mill a century earlier. He served the community as a part-time deputy sheriff, and was respected for his diplomacy and discretion in handling the job, which meant he could get a drunk and angry husband to go sleep it off, or quietly replace the item an older resident just may have accidentally slipped into a pocket. On the day he died a hero, Daniel, the oldest of Tom's four sons, came home from school to find himself the man of the household.

The emergency sirens at the steel mill shrilled through the morning air and the entire town held its breath. By the end of the day, everyone knew that Thomas MacBride was dead and two others, Andrew Wiggins and Martin Miller, were critically injured. A weld let loose on the smelter, sending the steaming bucket of molten metal swinging free above and behind the heads of Wiggan and Miller. They couldn't see it but heard the snap and turned. MacBride, the foreman, saw it coming straight for his men and knocked them out of the way with a diving tackle. A side swipe from the bucket drove his head into an iron support bar.

Sorrow at his untimely loss settled over the valley like a disquieting fog, seeping into every household.

At the MacBride house, Daniel sat with his brothers, the 13-year-old twins Tom and Tim and 10-year-old Mikey, and their mother, Ellen, around the kitchen table, staring at the empty seat at the head. The phone in the hallway rang and rang, until Ellen got up and unplugged the cord from the wall. She held her boys' hands and they prayed. After a few hours, as if suddenly aware of the time, she got up and fixed supper. As she set each plate in front of them, she gently placed her hand on their shoulders to let them know they were not alone.

Most of the food was still on the plates when the younger boys went to their rooms. Daniel and his mother huddled in the living room of the unusually quiet house. She reconnected the phone and began making calls to see what needed to be done to retrieve her husband's body from the hospital.

When the funeral was over, Daniel rode his bike to Kerin's Hill. His grandfather had immortalized his beloved wife, Kerin, by giving her name to it. And he had passed the land to Daniel, his oldest grandson and the one who had Kerin's eyes. The sun was warm on his face as the boy sat half hidden in the tall grasses, embraced by their long arms while bright daffodils and cornflowers swayed in the light breeze, singing their wind songs of comfort.

Most of the town, dressed in black, had come to the house after the funeral. He listened to their expressions of sympathy and reassuring comments as long as he could. "Everything will be all right, son." "We're so sorry, Daniel." "Things will work out, boy."

He clenched his fists so tightly that his fingernails had broken the skin of his palms until they bled. Sure, things would be fine for them. When the shock wore off, they'd go on with their lives. But Daniel wouldn't. His mother would still be a widow trying to raise her sons on a meager pension. His brothers would still look to him as the oldest to take care of them. His dreams of going to college and playing football had died with his dad. Damn him for being a dead hero to everybody else instead of a living father to his sons.

There was a whisper of parting grasses. He had seen the girl standing across the street from the house, arms resting on her bike's handlebars. He had seen her at the church, in the last row. After that, he had looked for her at the cemetery and finally spotted her, standing half hidden behind a tree, watching. Now she sat down beside him and pulled her knees up, just as he had, and wrapped her thin arms around them.

He knew who she was, of course, although he'd never really spoken to her. He was football; she was chess club. He was putting together a band; she was, well, a geek. His face stiffened. Melissa Sullivan lived with her aunt, Mimi Witherspoon, in that creepy house up on Witherspoon Lane. And the Witherspoons owned the mill that had killed his dad, didn't they?

Seeing his expression tighten, she murmured, "I'm sorry—for everything, Daniel." She added in a quiet melodic voice, "I'm sorry that your dad is gone and I'm sorry that I'm a Witherspoon. But I really do know how you feel."

He turned his head away. Everyone in school knew that her parents had been killed in a terrible accident. He looked at her, ready to push her away from him with a scathing insult, but then he met her eyes and recognized what he saw there. Pain. Compassion. Those golden-brown eyes really did understand how alone, abandoned, and angry he felt. He looked away and swallowed the lump in his throat.

He muttered a feeble, "Get lost, will ya?"

To his surprise, she stood and brushed the dirt off her jeans then said calmly, "Can I just tell you one more thing? It's really all I came to say."

"What?" He asked brusquely.

She laid a hand on his shoulder and leaned down to whisper in his ear in a voice almost as pained as his own. "It does get easier. I wanted you to know that."

Then he heard her bike tires on the grass.

After he was sure she was gone, Daniel put his head down on his arms and cried.

Daniel shook his head to clear the memory out of it. *Melissa.* He prayed to God he wouldn't have to explain to her how he felt after they had made love. Hadn't they been through enough? Then he took a deep breath and prayed for Sally, wherever she was.

CHAPTER TWENTY

Sally's disappearance was big news and the whole town had heard it by now, even Melissa. Donna, her best friend from high school and Sally's supervisor at the hospital gift shop, had called first thing. Melissa hadn't been fond of Sally. Not many girls in town were. She was well-known as the one who gave most of the boys their first experiences in backseat sex. Melissa had suspected that Daniel might be among them.

She put it out of her mind and decided she was just going stir crazy so she got out her running shoes. Her thoughts tumbled over each other as she pounded along, paying no attention to her direction because it was hard to get lost around Sylvan Mills. As she slowed down and grabbed her water bottle, she realized she was on Old Airport Road, standing in front of a banged up mailbox with the name Walters barely visible in faded paint outlines. An equally grim-looking old trailer stood behind it at the end of a gravel driveway overgrown with grass.

She wasn't crazy about the idea of walking through the trashy yard, but Melissa desperately wanted to knock on that door. She was naturally curious. She might also be avoiding working on her new book or escaping Jane's hopeful face. Or she might be looking for something to take her mind off her own personal situation. She nodded to herself. Okay, her motives might not be pure but she was okay with that. Besides, she was here.

She untied the handkerchief from around her forehead and wiped her face. As she recalled, Sally's dad was a nasty old drunk, one to avoid as he stumbled down the streets of town, making his labored way home. He talked to himself and didn't like to be interrupted.

Melissa thought about how best to approach him. She needed an angle, something that would justify intruding on the old guy. Well, she was a writer. *Research—her next book—that was good.* She was picking her way carefully through the junky yard when the dingy metal door opened and a shaggy grey head popped out.

"Ain't buyin', lady. Ain't givin', neither."

She smiled a trustworthy smile. "Lord, Mr. Walters, I'm not collecting or selling." She stuck out a hand. "Melissa Sullivan. You probably don't remember me. I went to high school here."

He rubbed at the scrawny beard on his chin. "Know the name. Wrote a book, din't ya? It was in the paper." He scowled at the surprise on her face. "I kin read, ya know."

"Of course." She shrugged and withdrew her hand. "Um, I was just out jogging."

"This ain't no pit stop."

She chuckled. "I know. When I saw your trailer, I thought I'd see if I could talk to you about Sally."

He eyed her with suspicion and scratched himself casually. "How come?"

She wished she had a better answer; the old man looked like he knew a lie when he heard one. "Well, since you already know I'm a writer, I guess I was thinking I might use something of Sally's story in my new book." She was aware of how selfish and heartless that sounded. "But, most of all, I'd like to help you find her. We weren't friends; I'm not gonna lie to you. But I hope she's okay. That's the truth."

After looking her over for another moment, he nodded. "Comeonin." He disappeared inside and she followed him. *Poor Sally. Who could blame her for running away from this dump?* Actually, it would have been understandable if she'd burned the thing down before she left. The old man settled himself into a chair at the kitchen table and she followed suit, carefully avoiding putting her arms on the sticky tabletop by folding her hands in her lap and trying to keep the back of her bare legs off the questionable material beneath her.

The watery blue eyes settled on her face. "So, how come ya think ya kin do better'n the cops, missy?"

She smiled at his accidental use of her old nickname. "Sometimes the police are hard to talk to. They get an idea of what might have happened and don't keep an open mind. Sometimes it's easier to talk without the pressure of a uniform. You know?"

He reached behind him without standing and pulled a beer out of the refrigerator. "Wanna cold one?"

Melissa smiled. "Don't mind if I do. Thanks."

While Johnny pulled two bottles out of the refrigerator, Melissa looked around. Her glance landed on a photo in a frame, a family shot of a young man in army uniform with a cocky grin, a blonde little girl by his side. When he returned, she looked at him a little differently. As they say on TV, she thought, every person has a story.

Half an hour and two cold ones later, she stood up, her head throbbing. "Do you, uh, mind if I look at her room?"

"Hell, no. Reckon ya don't need to steal nothin'. But the po-lice already been." He pointed to a door in the hallway, as he walked over to turn up the volume on the black and white TV and settled onto the sagging couch.

The hair on the back of her neck stood up as she opened the door. The room was small but surprisingly neat. She pulled open a drawer reeking of sachet and found a few sets of neatly folded underwear. It was oddly touching to see Sally's cheap dresses and skirts hung tidily in the closet. She sat down on the chenille spread with its rose-flowered pattern and tried to think like Sally. Where would she hide something?

When she returned to the living room, the old man hadn't moved. "Mr. Walters, did Sally keep a diary? A date book? A calendar of some kind?"

He bristled. "Kin call me John. And my girl didn't book 'em by the hour or nothin'."

"No, no. That's not what I meant, er, John, but a lot of girls, women, keep a diary or a journal. Just to remember special moments, special dates, stuff like that."

He shifted, pulled an empty bottle from beneath him and dropped it on the floor. "Not that I know of." He hesitated. "But I been thinkin' 'bout the liberry. She was one for goin' to the liberry. I'm thinkin' she mighta used one a them computers they got over there."

"Sally used a computer?" Before he could retort, she said, "I'm sorry. It's just that I didn't know. Please, cut me a break. I'm trying to help here."

He sat back against the drooping cushions.

She pressed on, thinking out loud. "She probably put her stuff on a disk that she could carry with her. Did you ever see one around? It would look like this. Or a CD?" She held her hands out first in a small square, then a larger circle.

He actually laughed out loud. "I got TV, woman. I know what them things looks like, for chrissake."

Melissa laughed with him. "Okay. Help me find it then."

CHAPTER TWENTY-ONE

The damned thing about broke her heart. It had all but burned a hole in her pocket the whole way back home. She couldn't explain why she hadn't told Johnny that she found it. She didn't intend to explain why she hadn't rushed over to the police with it. It didn't feel right.

The disk contained page after page of Sally's life. It was far too easy to imagine her typing furiously and then secreting it away. There was certainly no one in this town she could have told these things to and had them remain private.

It went back to the tenth grade when Sally figured it out.

> I'm the girl who gives it up so easy. They think they're using me. It's too easy to get what I want. I'm using them.

Melissa remembered hearing that Sally had told a few other girls that the school jock was "disappointing" and regaled them with stories of his "shortcomings." That episode was recounted in detail.

> I told the truth. Big deal. So then he gives me looks that could kill in the school hall the next day. Joan and Beth actually spoke to me when they passed me. It was still a good day.

My God, she even made it with a few of the teachers and named names. Melissa felt her heart start to race. These were family men no doubt still teaching.

It's so funny, the way the married guys are so afraid to get caught, I've got nothing to lose but they've got everything. As far as I'm concerned, they can afford to spend a little more to go out of town and take me to a decent restaurant. And I know that if they get caught, they'll blame me. The assholes. They think they're using me – but they're wrong. Everybody's wrong. I do what I do to get things I need and will never have otherwise. A girl like me don't have many choices. So for half an hour of my life, they get to feel like a man. I know their girlfriends and wives hate me but they're the ones dumb enough to hook up with these guys. All the girls in this town think about is Tupperware parties and football games and then babies.

There was even a page or two where she wondered if life would have been different if her mother hadn't left her. At one point, Melissa gasped out loud.

Nobody is supposed to know but I'm sure Momma was sleeping with Garrett Anniston. Boy, wouldn't that put his boxers in a twist if that got out! That bitch of a wife of his would cut his balls off. I don't think that's why Momma run away, not totally. Dad's been messed up for a long time. I seen a picture of him in his uniform and he was a good looking man. I think Momma got tired of being disappointed. You can be sure old Anniston wasn't about to dump his rich wife and marry the likes of her. So she gave up and took off. I wish she'd taken me with her. I surely do.

Melissa let her breath out slowly. There were enough names, dates, and places in here to literally blow Sylvan Mills to high heaven and back. This was interesting.

> *MOMD* [man of my dreams] *let slip a big secret. I had a bit too much and told Danny M. He made me promise not to tell anyone. He scared me. I'm not even gonna write it down in case somebody gets a hold of this. I'm not sure if it's because he still cares about her or because it would blow the lid off this town if it got out.*

She thought about that for a minute and then skimmed along to the last few pages.

> *We went over to Brookville to that new restaurant last night. It was so fancy. I had a fillet mignon, which is a steak. He had lobster, can't say I care for it. We are going to the Hilton in Scranton for the weekend, room service and everything.*

Sally went on about their adventures together. Then he started giving her things.

> *MOMD gave me a golden heart on a chain but said I should probably not wear it around town. That's okay. I don't mind. He has to think about his career and our future. He told me he loves me but I should never ever tell anyone, not even Dad, until the time is right. When you work in government and politics, you have to be real careful.*

Melissa felt tears welling in her eyes. Dear Lord, Sally thought that some local politician was going to marry the girl that everyone looked past on the street. Her naiveté was almost unbelievable.

> *People around here think I give it all away. Well, I'm about to get it all back and then some. I've worked hard and I've earned it. I am gonna have me a beautiful house and a bunch of kids. They won't want for nothing, ever. Maybe we can get Dad into rehab, even. I know there's some as won't believe it but I'm in LOVE. And now for the best part. I took a pregnancy test this morning and it was POSITIVE. I'm having his baby. Now he's sure to pop the question. I can't wait to tell him.*

After she regained her composure, she stashed the disk carefully in her laptop case.

She thought seriously about turning it over to the police but what good would it do? How would they be able to track down MOMD? The poor girl probably thought she'd jinx it if she wrote her boyfriend's name down in black and white. No one really knew for certain that she hadn't simply gone out of town for a couple of days.

Melissa made a decision to keep the disk for now and see what happened. If Sally showed up, she'd just return the disk to her somehow without letting her know she'd read it. And she'd figure out a way to ask her about the "dirty little secret"—unless she got it out of Daniel first.

It might be said that Melissa had published her own personal diary for the world to see when she wrote her book, but truth be told she couldn't bear the thought of anyone else, especially the police, rummaging through Sally's sad little hopes and dreams. edit

CHAPTER TWENTY-TWO

Energized by her trip to the Walters' trailer and relieved by her decision to hold onto Sally's diary, Melissa grabbed Jane's shopping list and took off to the local supermarket. Her ulterior motive was simple: after several days of meat and potatoes, vegetables and salad fixings were high on the list. She felt like she had gained five pounds since she'd gotten here.

Asparagus? Jane allowed to having heard of it but had never cooked or served it. Kale was a mystery; brussel sprouts just sounded so "foreign".

At the store, while sorting through a pile of tomatoes, she accidentally shoved her shopping cart into another one.

The woman on the other side of the cart looked up from the cucumbers. "Melissa?"

Melissa searched her memory frantically. "Jill? Jillian Hawkins?"

"I heard you were home," The girl said with a nod.

"How are you? It's been a long time." The petite blonde looked even more fragile than she remembered.

"Since we blew up that science experiment and got suspended?" She smiled shyly.

"For sure. I got in a few days ago." Melissa smiled back. "Hey, wanna have lunch and you can fill me in on what's happening here in town?"

"Nothing much ever happens around here." Jill sighed. "I bet your life in New York City's real excitin', huh?"

Melissa laughed. "Not always, but sometimes a little too much."

"Well, my boy's in school so, uh, sure, why not? Let me get my groceries home and put away and I'll meet you at

O'Malley's around one, is that okay? You remember O'Malley's?"

"Are you kidding? See you there." She hurried through her shopping.

When she walked into the diner, Melissa was given the once-over by some young guys sitting on the stools in front of the counter. One of them in particular seemed familiar to her. He slid into the booth across from her.

"Guess I've grown some, huh?"

"Mike! Omigod. Yeah. You were, like, four feet tall last time I saw you. Now you're all grown up and gorgeous!"

She grabbed his hands and leaned across to peck his cheek. Mike MacBride pulled back, embarrassed, and started talking. He worked at the mill now and was a volunteer fireman.

When Jill hurried in, Mike quickly muttered something that sounded like "Seeya" and went back to the stool at the counter.

Melissa turned her attention to Jill. "So tell me about your little boy. Kevin? How old is he?"

"Eight, he'll be nine in October."

"Wow."

"Yeah, I can hardly believe it myself." Jill leaned forward eagerly. "But I'd much rather hear all about you."

"Well, let's see. I work for a newspaper in the city, where I share an apartment with a charming psychologist, and I'm writing my second novel."

The little blonde actually clapped her hands together. "Oh, Melissa, that sounds so glamorous."

Melissa laughed. "You know, it does sound that way. But believe me, there's a lot of work involved in all three."

After they placed their order, there was a brief silence, and then Jill's big blue eyes grew serious. "You heard about Sally, I suppose?"

Melissa answered carefully. "I'm not sure exactly what you mean."

"Her goin' missing and all." She paused and then added firmly, "Sam had nothin' to do with it. He liked Sally. We all did."

"Sam? You mean Sam Gray?"

Jill nodded shyly. "My husband."

"You married Sam Gray?" Melissa's face, as usual, showed what she thought.

"You probably didn't know it but ... our senior year of high school, Sam got me pregnant." She took a drink of water. "This is still a small town, Melissa, and getting married was the right thing to do." She hesitated again, then her face brightened. "Kevin is a great boy, I can't imagine being without him. And Sam makes a decent living, we have our own home. It's really not so bad, mostly." She sighed. "That sounds lame, I know. But we don't all have as many choices as you did."

The thought of this petite woman living with Sam Gray put a damper on the mood. Jill kept asking her questions and Melissa tried to answer coherently. Just as their lunches were placed in front of them, there was a ruckus at the door of the restaurant.

Melissa looked toward the noise. "Well, speak of the devil."

Jill cringed as her husband strode over, grabbed her arm roughly, and pulled her out of the booth. "What the hell are you doing here, woman? Haven't you got enough to do at home?"

He propelled her toward the door, her feet barely touching ground.

"Wait a minute." Melissa pushed off the bench seat and followed. "Look, Sam, I haven't seen Jill in a long time and we were just having lunch."

He pointed a beefy finger at her face. "No, you look. She don't need you fillin' her head with your big city ideas. See? So don't come near her again."

Melissa was fuming. "Why you ignorant ape. How dare you?"

From behind him, Jill cried out, "Please, Melissa, let it go."

Melissa was still surprised when he raised his hand. She recovered quickly and spoke in a loud clear voice. "Hey, everybody. Mr. Macho here is about to deck me. I'll need several witnesses for my assault and battery charges so make sure you get a good look." She glared at him and said, "Smack away, pal, and I'll be more than happy to see you put in a cage where you belong."

Grumbling erupted from the onlookers and suddenly Mike and several others stood between them. Someone grabbed Sam's arm. "Come on, Sam, she ain't worth it." Giving Melissa one more furious look, the big man turned and hauled Jill out the door.

Melissa moved to follow but Mike took her arm. "Geez, Melissa, what are you, suicidal?"

Melissa turned on him. "What the hell kind of town lets an animal like that roam the streets?" She stormed out of the diner, down the street, and up the hill.

She closed the door to the police station with a bang. "I'd like to speak to someone now!"

"Chief's here but he's busy right now, ma'am." A flush started to spread up rookie Rich Farrell's neck.

"I'll wait, but not long." She stared him down.

The young cop picked up the phone while Melissa paced back and forth, keeping her steam up.

When Rich whispered into the phone that Melissa was waiting out front, Daniel took a deep breath, opened the door, and stood in the doorway. "Come on in. Something I can do for you?"

Oh crap, Daniel. How could it have slipped her mind? *Awkward. Too bad.* She wanted someone to do something about Sam Gray. This was official police business. She marched past him into his office. "Damn straight."

He shrugged in the direction of Rich's wide eyes and followed her into his office. He sat down behind his desk and, in order to keep a straight face, tried not to watch Melissa pace in front of it while muttering nasty words. She was so damned cute, marching back and forth in her yellow-flowered sundress, white ankle socks, and sneakers. He brought himself back to earth: *Jennifer*. At least now he could say he had seen Melissa when she came to the station. It wouldn't be a lie.

He let her rant for a few minutes and then leaned forward. "Hello? I haven't got all day."

She leaned over the desk, her outraged face even with his. For a split second she remembered ... yesterday. He leaned back, away from her.

"Sam Gray is the problem. How can you let him treat Jill like that? Why is he still loose on the streets? I could just ..." She clenched a fist in frustration and banged it down on the desk.

He sighed. "So you've run into Sam. I figured you would sooner or later. I was hoping for later. Would you like some coffee or a soda?"

She spoke through clenched teeth. "No, thank you."

"Well, I do. So cool your heels for a couple of minutes. You have lunch?"

Melissa exploded. "I was trying to have lunch with Jill. That's what I'm telling you."

He held up both hands, not sure if it was a sign of surrender or a sign of authority. "I can't hear you when you're screaming at me. Okay? Okay." He opened the door. "Hey, Rich, order us a couple of subs from across the street, vinegar and oil, not mayonnaise, couple of sodas, maybe some chips. Thanks."

"Oh, for God's sake."

He turned. "Sit down, Melissa, and listen to me."

She did as she was told, although she had no idea why. Between what had happened yesterday and the fact that it hadn't seemed to affect him at all, she was awfully confused. What the hell was he smiling at?

The grin had finally escaped.

"Stop that. It confuses me. There's absolutely nothing funny about this."

He sobered up fast. "I'm painfully aware of that."

"Can't you do something, Daniel? I want to press charges." She glared at him and smacked her fist on his desk again. "I want you to lock him up and throw away the damned key."

He covered a chuckle by clearing his throat. "And what are the charges? Being an asshole? What did he do to you?"

"He pissed me off. But that's not the problem. It's Jill. He treats her like ... like he owns her!"

He nodded. "Let me guess. You and Jill were chatting up old times and he showed up and dropkicked her out the door, something like that?"

Melissa was running out of steam. "More or less."

The door opened and the young cop, color still high, handed over several brown bags. "I got you a couple of those warm chocolate chip cookies you like, chief." He nodded at Melissa. "Ma'am." Seeing Daniel busy removing packages from the bags, he leaned toward Melissa and almost whispered, "Is it true that you offered to let Sam Gray deck you?"

She nodded and flashed him a grin.

Daniel stopped unwrapping sandwiches. "You did what?" He glared at Melissa.

The door slammed with the rookie safely on the other side of it, but not before he gave Melissa a quick thumbs-up.

"Well, I didn't start it. It was his idea to hit me."

"What did he do and exactly what did you say?" He kept his voice calm.

"He raised his hand to hit me. I simply asked the people around us, including your brother Mike, to pay attention so they could be witnesses in my assault and battery case. I told him to swing away and I'd see to it that he was put into a cage where he belongs." Daniel's face paled. She shrugged. "Well, he does."

He covered his face with his hands for a moment.

"I was mad, Daniel. He's a Neanderthal." She was working her way back to fury. "I couldn't just let him get away with that shit. I couldn't."

"Will you stop already, for God's sake? You've ruined my lunch." He put down the sandwich. "This will be all over town by now."

"So?"

"You've been away too long, Melissa. Think about it. You just publicly humiliated the biggest bully in the county. You think he can let you get away with that?"

"So what's he gonna do? Flatten my tires?"

A look flickered across his face and she remembered what Sam was capable of ...

Books scattered on the ground ... commotion behind a car in the parking lot ... a muffled cry ... Donna's red hair... tears streaming down her face ... Sam's hand on her neck holding her down ...

"I see you remember high school." Daniel sighed. "He was bad then and it's been straight downhill for Sam ever since, Melissa. He's made some nasty friends. You saved Donna back then because it was daylight in a public place; who's going to be around to save you when he sneaks up on you some night?"

"Okay, okay, I get it. I embarrassed the bastard and shouldn't be hanging around dark alleys." She straightened her shoulders. "But he hurts her, you can bet on it. And they have a little boy, Daniel." She jumped up and started pacing again. "No one should have to live that way."

He walked around the desk, stood in her path, and tried a gentler tone. "Listen to me. Jill won't press charges."

"He'd probably kill her if she did."

"It's a distinct possibility."

"But ..."

"Off the record, Tom and I have kicked the crap out of him a couple of times. That doesn't work, either."

Frustration took some of the fire out of her eyes. "So we wait until he kills her to have the evidence to stop him?"

"Unless I can come up with another reason to lock him up."

He let her think while he sat down and started on his sandwich again.

"Like whatever's happened to Sally," she said slowly while looking at the floor. "Jill says he had nothing to do with it."

Did he know she had been at the Walters' trailer? Well, if he thought he was going to blackmail her into revealing what she'd found, he could just think again.

He put his sandwich down again, "Really?"

She studied her shoes. "So, if I talk Jill into leaving him, where can she go?"

He shoved his sandwich aside and gave her his hardest policeman glare. He had thought for sure she was about to tell him what she was doing at the Walters' trailer.

He raised his hands as if to put them on her shoulders to look her in the eye, and then dropped them heavily to his sides. Yesterday was there in his eyes for a moment, then gone. His voice was hard.

"Are you deaf? He will then kill both of you and probably me when I try to bring him in. Listen, if it makes you feel any better, the bastard only gets really nasty when he gets drunk and that's mostly on Friday nights. So that's when I cruise by the house a few times. Sometimes I stop in to say hello. Sometimes weeks go by and nothing happens. She's the only one who gives a damn about him, don't look at me that way because she does, and that's exactly why he doesn't want you around her. He's afraid you'll talk her into leaving him. You have to think of Jill first, Melissa. You do anything to interfere, she's gonna pay for it. Let me handle it. I kinda have my hands full right now."

"Fine. But we're not done here." She pulled her eyes away from his and slammed the door behind her.

Daniel stood there. "No, we're not done." He whispered to the suddenly very quiet office.

CHAPTER TWENTY-THREE

Daniel was closing the door, ready to sign out, when Lou Vinterra slouched up alongside him.

Without looking up, Daniel spoke to his least favorite officer. "Lou. What's up?"

"I'd like to speak to you in private, chief, if you don't mind."

"Sure but I've only got a few minutes. Come on in." Daniel opened the door and went behind his desk, settling in his squeaky wooden chair. "Take a seat."

"Rather not."

Daniel leaned back and looked up at the man who should have had his job. The retiring chief had ignored Lou's experience and seniority to recommend Daniel as his replacement. After the initial shock wore off, most of the town had recognized it as a good call. It might have been unfair; Lou had never been charged with a crime. But, somehow, rumors and whispers persisted that any cousin of Max Vinterra's simply had to be crooked. Daniel recognized that Lou, if he was clean, had a right to be bitter. Still, they both counted the months until Lou's retirement.

"I'm the one Johnny Walters talked to about Sally." Lou shifted his weight.

Daniel nodded. "I figured."

"It wasn't even 24 hours, chief."

Daniel remained silent.

The man straightened up and put his hands out to Daniel, pleading. "For chrissake, chief, you know Sally. Probably took off with a trucker. The old man didn't have a thing to go on and he was drunk on his ass when he came in."

His whining further irritated an already irritated man. "You know damn well Sally wouldn't take off and leave the old man alone. She always goes home. And Johnny's been a drunk for years, you also know that, and it didn't mean what he was saying wasn't true."

Daniel caught himself raising his voice and regained control. He continued in a quieter, yet no less stern, tone. "None of us gets to make the call on who's important and who's not, what's real and what isn't. You should have filled out the report with whatever you had, signed it, and put it on the daily sheet so we could have checked it out or at least followed up quicker."

Lou looked down at his shoes and his hands fell to his sides. "I know. I know." He paused. "Give me that report back and I'll run with it and write it up proper, I swear."

"I don't think so. I'll handle it myself from here on." Daniel opened a folder in dismissal.

The old resentment flickered across the older man's face but he gave it one more shot. "Come on, Daniel. I know we haven't seen eye-to-eye on things around here, but there's no need to make me look bad over this. I'll go the distance on it, you have my word."

"You had your chance." Daniel looked at his watch. "I've gotta go. You better go make your rounds, Lou. It's getting late."

Settled in his car, Lou picked up his cell phone. "It's me." He listened intently and then replied on the defensive. "I had to eat it and I can still taste it." He listened another moment. "I tried to slow it down for you and now my ass is in a sling here. He's got it and he won't let go. This is your mistake. I'll do what I can but I am not gonna blow my pension for you, Max, you hear me?" With that, he closed his phone and threw it on the seat.

CHAPTER TWENTY-FOUR

As she walked home, Melissa's cell phone chimed. Donna announced firmly that they needed a night out. She instructed Melissa to meet her at the Wayside Tavern around nine. It never occurred to Melissa to argue with her. It never had.

First, though, she had dinner at the house. Mimi had been making an effort to join her and Jane at the table. She'd start about an hour before, dressing and making her way downstairs, resting in the living room until dinner was ready. Then she'd take her seat at the table. She didn't blink at the appearance of a salad and asparagus alongside the pork chops, fried potatoes, and biscuits. She didn't take any, either. Jane did her best to make casual conversation, but neither Melissa nor Mimi appeared to be in a particularly talkative mood. Eventually, more interesting topics emerged.

"So, Melissa, have you heard any news about Sally Walters?"

Both Melissa and Mimi looked up in surprise at Jane's blunt question.

She shrugged. "Well, we can't pretend we don't know she's missing. It's all over town."

"I heard she was pregnant," Mimi responded with a smirk.

"No!" Jane put a hand to her breast. "My, my, that poor girl."

Mimi chortled. "Apparently old Johnny tried to file a missing persons report and got thrown out of the police station for his trouble." She looked at Melissa.

Melissa was shocked by this casual exchange of gossip between her aunts. She had never imagined such a thing. But she refused to be baited into discussing Daniel and gave what she hoped would be a sufficient, if bland, response.

"Well, I hope she's okay. I think I'll skip dessert and get ready. I'm going out with Donna for a while. Excuse me." Melissa escaped to her room to get dressed for her girl's night out.

As soon as she walked in, Donna's call across the bar put an end to all other conversation. "Yoo-hoo, Melissa. Over here!" Melissa reminded herself of all the reasons she loved Donna, even though she found her a bit much—too loud, too fast, too much hair, and too much makeup. Melissa had been drawn to the bubbly Donna back in high school because of that very exuberance and, mostly, by her confidence. *Opposites attract.* She moved quickly across the room and slid into the booth beside her friend.

"Thanks for the entrance, Donna," Melissa whispered into her ear.

Her friend's laugh sent another shock wave through the place and Melissa winced. "Sure thing, honey. You always were a little stiff. It's good for you."

As two young women in tight jeans sashayed past their booth to take a table closer to the small bandstand, she teased Melissa unmercifully. "Whoo-hee, the one on the left is Daniel's fi-an-cee, remember Jennifer Murphy? I'll just bet she's tickled to death to see you. Watch your back, kiddo. Like I told you on the phone, you're the talk of the town, my dear, and our darling Jennifer doesn't like it at all. Her wedding was the big news until you showed up. She finally torments the poor bastard into making an honest woman out of her and then you come home and its game over. We are all watchin' with great an-ti-ci-pa-shun."

"But ..."

Donna clamped her hand over Melissa's mouth dramatically. "Oh, puh-leeze, don't even think of ruining this for me." After Melissa playfully nipped her palm, she chattered away for a few minutes, pointing out people in the room, and then Donna's brother, Jeff and his friend, Ronnie, joined them. Melissa wasn't sure exactly when, but at some point Howard Everett was there too. It occurred to Melissa that it had always been that way whenever they hung out, Howard was just there. He wasn't related to any of them, nor was he particularly friends with any of them, yet he had always been one of their gang. He was an average man now, just as he'd been an average boy, quiet and shy, his average brown hair already thinning. Melissa felt a wave of sympathy as she caught him looking at the bubbly Donna with a surprisingly tender expression.

"Do you know who's playin' tonight?" Donna asked Melissa innocently.

"How the heck would I know?"

Just then a door to the left of the small stage opened and Donna giggled. "Surprise!"

The guys walking out on stage were Daniel, Tom, and Mike MacBride. Melissa set her drink down carefully. That certainly explained Jennifer being front and center, guarding her turf, so to speak. Melissa was surprised she wasn't wearing an "I'm with the band" T-shirt.

Donna poked her in the ribs. "If you could only see your face!"

Time flew by and it felt like most of the town passed through the Wayside Tavern. The band was in perfect tune with the audience and filled the room with gentle rock and memories of their "glory days." Faces and names and memories flew by in a blur. It was almost closing time and she had just decided it was time to go when she felt a hand on her shoulder. She looked up to see Jennifer standing there wearing a pained smile.

"Hi, Melissa, can I talk to you for a minute?"

"Uh, sure." Melissa scooted out of the booth and followed the smaller girl outside.

Melissa noted the fidgeting hand movements and the chewed nails. But Jennifer's eyes, when she raised them to Melissa's, were determined and defiant. "I know that you and Daniel used to have a thing for each other."

Melissa opened her mouth to protest but Jennifer shook her head.

"Please. Let's not waste each other's time. I just wanted to say this to your face now that you're back. He's mine. I've always loved him and I've waited for years ..." Her voice trembled and her eyes went glassy but she pushed her chin up and continued. "Our wedding is booked and it's going to happen. So I would appreciate it if you would ... just leave him alone."

Melissa let her breath out in a long exhale. She couldn't think of a thing to say that would be an honest response so she nodded. "I hear you."

Jennifer looked dubious. She cleared her throat. "You may be all big city, rich and famous and everything, but all I've ever wanted was to stay right here and have a home and a family." She raised a hand and poked her index finger in Melissa's shoulder. "You don't get to walk back in and take that away from me. Not without a fight." Jennifer face was flushed as she turned and walked quickly back into the bar before Melissa could respond.

Melissa stood in the quiet air for a few minutes before joining her friends. Seeing the subdued look on her face, Donna, showing remarkable sensitivity, gave her a hug and then glanced over at Howard. "Uh, do you mind if we call it a night?"

Melissa took the hint and waved her away. "Go, go. I'm gonna finish my beer and then I'm heading out too."

Jeff asked Melissa if she wanted him and Ronnie to wait for her.

"Nah, I know the way. Good night, fellas."

After they left, Melissa enjoyed the peace of being alone for about a minute and a half before a guy with black hair, blue eyes, and a smile that ended in deep dimples slid in beside her. "I know, I know. You're tired. You just want to finish your drink and go home."

"Are you a psychic by profession or avocation?" Melissa pushed her hair back wearily.

He responded without hesitation. "Just an overworked and underpaid doctor who's flattered that you feel comfortable using the word 'avocation" in a sentence and assuming I'll understand it."

Melissa laughed out loud. "Okay, you have my attention." She stuck out a hand. "Melissa Sullivan."

"I know. Jake Capelli. If I go away now and leave you alone, would you consider having dinner with me tomorrow night?"

Melissa considered; she could use some intelligent conversation and he had really nice eyes. Maybe the beer and smoke had gone to her head but she nodded.

"Great. I'll call you." He slid away without asking for her number. Oh, well, it was probably for the best. *Like she needed more men in her life.*

She finished her beer and headed for home.

Daniel eased his guitar case into the Jeep. She was almost ready to leave before the new doctor took his shot and it looked like they hit it off, all that nodding and smiling. Daniel slammed his hand against the steering wheel before he remembered it was none of his business.

Or was Melissa his business, literally? She had been snooping around out at the Walters place. If she knew anything she wasn't telling him, well, he ought to try to get it out of her, right? *Just doing his job.*

Melissa was slowly walking home, wondering what was wrong with her anyway, feeling disloyal to Stephen not only for her interlude with Daniel, but for agreeing to dinner with the cute doctor. *What's wrong with me?*

Daniel pulled up alongside her, bringing on a deep stab of outright guilt. She ignored him.

"Melissa." He called her name softly.

Well, that worked well. She stopped. "So what's goin' on?"

"Why don't you tell me?"

"Still answering a question with a question, chief? One of these days you're gonna give me a straight answer and I'm gonna keel right over." Melissa's head ached and her eyes were not used to smoky taverns. She squinted at him. "Is that a smile or are you in some kind of pain?"

The grin widened.

"I gotta get home and sleep it off." She started walking again.

"I might as well drop you off."

Melissa was bewildered and embarrassed by her conversation with Jennifer and just sober enough to be suspicious; he was still trying to get her to tell him she had been at Sally's trailer. He wouldn't give up. That helped. She concentrated on remembering the way he had treated her and on being pissed about it. That helped, too. "What do you want from me, Daniel?" She asked in what she hoped was a firm no-nonsense voice.

"I'd like a chance to explain. But I have a feeling this isn't the right time."

"And you'd be right. Not tonight. I have a headache." She looked him straight in the eye. "I'll walk, but thanks just the same."

He pulled away, but circled the block and followed her at a distance to make sure she got home safely.

CHAPTER TWENTY-FIVE

The next day, after sleeping in and making an attempt at some writing, Melissa wandered into the living room and stopped short. Mimi sat there, reading.

"Well, well, nice of you to stop by."

She sat down across from her aunt. "I've been in this house most of the time since I came back, Mimi. I can't stay in all the time."

"Hmmph." The book she had been reading plopped softly onto the sofa. "So you've been catching up with everyone?"

This attempt at civil conversation caught Melissa off guard. "Sort of."

"And how does your doctor feel about you being away so long?"

"He's a big boy. I've only been gone a few days."

Her aunt nodded. "Well, you're a very confident young woman." She hesitated. "I appreciate your visit, Melissa, truly. But I would not have you ruin your relationship while I ... linger." With that, she picked up her book and wouldn't look at Melissa again.

Melissa sat there for a moment then got up and walked out.

Jane Witherspoon looked up from stirring her sauce to see her niece's face wearing that crumpled expression that was all too familiar. Damn. She wished Mimi would make it easier for Melissa to want to help her. Still, she hadn't said "no"—yet.

"Let me guess. She's hurt your feelings." She put her plump arm around her taller niece and patted her back. "Come on. Sit down and take a load off."

Melissa sighed. "She wants me to leave. She all but said so."

"I don't believe it. Hold on a minute. I want to show you something." Jane came back holding a scrapbook. "She's still reading. Now here, you take a look at this."

Melissa opened it to find every letter or note she had written to her aunts, her graduation announcement, every newspaper story she had written, her book reviews. She let it fall shut. "You kept everything?"

Jane shook her head. "No, honey, she keeps everything. She even got a subscription to your newspaper so she could check for articles with your name on them. She loves you, Melissa, she always has."

Melissa stared at the book in front of her. "She has a funny way of showing it."

Jane's strained response came slowly. "Well, honey, there's a lot you don't know. Our father was a cold, hard man and he treated Mimi, who was the oldest, the worst. Then the only man she ever loved threw her away like she was nothing. She's never really recovered. Mimi's never felt loved, so how would she know how to show love to anyone else?"

Melissa thought it over. "How can you be so different?"

Jane chuckled. "Sweetie, I got out of here as soon as I was old enough. I had a life. It may have been a while ago now, but at least I have my memories."

"Aunt Jane, I have to ask, why on earth did you come back and why did you stay all these years?"

"Oh, you know. You came along. I was getting older and it was difficult to find a job. I needed a place to live. I suppose I could have taken off after you went to college but, after all, this is my home too." She flushed.

Melissa noticed. "Why Aunt Jane, you should see your face! Do you have a gentleman caller?"

"Never you mind," her red-faced aunt answered crisply.

Melissa hugged the little woman. "I'm just teasing you. And I don't tell you often enough how much I love you, Aunt Jane. You're the best."

"You stop it now or you'll have me all worked up."

Melissa grabbed a cookie from the always-full cookie jar on the kitchen counter and winked at her. "Oh, by the way, I'm going out to dinner. I have a date." Feeling a little lighter at the astonished look on Jane's face, she went upstairs to dress. She muttered under her breath, *at least I think I do, that is if the good doctor remembers and knows where I live.*

Jane sat down heavily at the kitchen table. It was none of her business if Melissa had a date. She put that away firmly. But the weight on her heart remained now that Melissa had brought it up. *Why had she stayed?* Because, when she was young and foolish, she had made her own mistakes.

She sat in her tiny kitchen in Chicago and let her tears drip on the plastic tablecloth. How could this have happened to her? She had landed a job in a chorus line, first step in her master plan to be a lead dancer in a musical. Three steps that she repeated like a mantra: line dancer, stand-in for the lead, the lead. Five years she'd been going to cattle calls, taking classes, sucking up the rejection, dismissal, and indifference of casting directors all over Chicago. She could have gone to New York but she wasn't good enough. She knew that.

So she had slept with a guy or two in the business. Everybody did that. But not everybody was dumb enough to get knocked up.

Her hand shook as she picked up the glass of vodka. She set it back down. Pregnant women shouldn't drink, right? The tears fell faster.

Abortion was out of the question; she just couldn't go there, so she toughed it out. The father was willing to help her financially as long as she kept her mouth shut. When she delivered, alone, a 7 pound 4 oz baby girl at Chicago General, she refused to see her.

A couple from California was taking her. The agency had provided references and background information that made them look like a solid choice.

Jane went home, alone. Four weeks later, she was back on auditions. She spent most of her time trying hard not to think about it.

Then Mimi called ... the number she had been given but had not used once in all those long years. The shock that she had actually called was bad enough, but when she asked for help that was unimaginable.

It was a conversation worth remembering. "I am calling with some terrible news, Jane. Emily's been killed. The service is day after tomorrow."

Jane gasped. "Oh, Lord."

"Indeed. Her husband was also in the accident. So, uh, the child will be coming to live here ... with me."

Jane gasped again. "Oh, no."

"Yes, I agree. However, this is the circumstance in which we find ourselves."

Jane finally exhaled. "My sweet Jesus." Her head was spinning. "But you can't possibly. I mean, how will you? Dear God!"

"I have been considering all options. I would ... appreciate your assistance, Jane." She managed in a more subdued tone than Jane had ever heard from her. "Well. She is eleven, almost twelve. She's not a baby. But still ..."

Jane sighed as understanding set in after the initial shock. "You want me to come back and help you with her because you don't have a maternal bone in your body." It was a statement not a question.

"Unless, of course, your dance career is finally taking off?" Mimi retaliated.

A slow smile crossed Jane's face. There was the big sister she had come to know ... and pretty much hate. But no child deserved to be raised by Mimi. The universe had decided that Jane was to help raise a girl child anyway, no matter what actions she might take to the contrary.

Jane Witherspoon heard Melissa bouncing up the stairs to get dressed for her dinner date. *Why had she stayed?* She could never tell her the truth. It was a matter of penance.

CHAPTER TWENTY-SIX

There wasn't much to choose from. She'd brought jeans and t-shirts, a black suit that would work for a funeral, and one other dress, her cream silk sheath and, thank God, the matching pumps. One thing Mimi had drilled into her was to pack a complete outfit. She found pearl earrings and a matching single strand necklace in her jewelry case. If she didn't get out of here soon, she would have to shop or call Stephen to send her more clothes. Mimi had made her point. She had to call him tomorrow. The question was— what would she say? Or maybe it was how much should she tell him?

She followed her aunts' voices into the living room, where Jake was charming them with kind words about the house, their lovely niece, the flowers outside, and everything he could think of, apparently. She rescued him quickly.

He gallantly installed her in the deep bucket seats of his vintage black Corvette, on which she complimented him with genuine delight.

He wiped his forehead with his handkerchief and settled behind the wheel. "Whoa."

She laughed. "Did I not mention the aunts?"

He shook his head and started the car.

They zoomed down the interstate and within ten minutes were walking into the restaurant Jake had chosen. The relaxed but elegant atmosphere impressed her. After they settled in with glasses of wine, he looked at Melissa appraisingly and she colored slightly under the scrutiny.

"What?"

The dimples deepened. "Just checking to make sure it was worth it."

She laughed out loud. "And?"

He shrugged. "So far, I have no complaints."

"I think I like you, Dr. Capelli."

"Can't fault your taste. Now tell me how a lovely, intelligent woman, who obviously has discerning taste in men, comes to be in Sylvan Mills, Pennsylvania."

"I was born here."

"Ahh. I seem to remember a guy at the bar saying something about a local girl who just came back home. So you apparently got out and, what, returned voluntarily?" He faked horror.

She chuckled. "Not exactly." She explained about her aunt being ill, glossing over the background details.

"So you expect to be leaving."

"Yes, soon."

"And I'm guessing there's a guy waiting."

"Pretty much." She felt herself flushing.

"And what about our esteemed chief of police?"

Melissa almost choked on her wine. "What about him?"

The blue eyes were warm on her face for a brief moment before he shrugged and signaled the waiter.

After they had ordered, Melissa started the conversation again. "So, Jake, you've heard my excuse. What brings you here?"

"I thought you'd never ask. Talking about myself is my second favorite thing to do." He raised his eyebrows suggestively. "My dad, actually, is responsible for my exile in this bucolic community."

She raised an eyebrow in return.

"Intrigued? Good. My dad went to Penn State and remembers the area with great fondness. When I had to intern, he suggested the rural experience. Voila, I am a proud member of the staff of Community Hospital. I work at the clinic too."

"Because your father told you to?"

"Because he paid for medical school, my dear. Until I'm practicing on my own, I have no problem humoring the old guy. And I wanted to see what it would be like. Once I get my medical license, then I'll have to decide where I want to practice, city or country?"

She nodded. "Do you like being a doctor?"

"Sometimes, actually, most of the time. The babies are the best."

Melissa blinked. "What kind of doctor are you?"

"Here it comes." He grinned. "Ob-Gyn."

"Oh."

"You know, I almost always get that response. Please try not to hold it against me."

She shook her head. It did make a difference, although she wasn't sure just why.

The 'vette roared to a halt in front of her house before she knew it and she turned to face him with a twinkle in her eye. "Care to come in?"

His gaze went to the house. "I don't think so."

She followed his glance to the big Victorian. "I don't blame you. I wish I didn't have to go in, either."

"If we were going to continue to see each other, I would suggest my apartment next time."

"If?"

"Don't be coy. It's not your style. We had a good time, I like you, you like me." He sighed exaggeratedly. "But I have a fairly clear sense of these things, and I think I've come on to the field too late to take the competition."

"I do like you, doc," she said. "It's just that my life's very confusing right now."

"If you get unconfused, you know how to find me."

She leaned over and kissed him firmly on the cheek. "Good night, doc."

"Good night, lovely lady," he said with a grin. "Sweet dreams."

As he sped away, he found himself wondering if all the good ones were taken.

CHAPTER TWENTY-SEVEN

After breakfast the next morning, Melissa called Stephen. The phone rang several times and she was about to hang up, not wanting to leave another voice mail, when he picked up.

"Thank you for finding the time to call me, Melissa." He answered in his professional voice.

"I'm sorry, Stephen." She twisted the kitchen wall phone's yellow cord around her fingers. She had felt like using the house phone instead of her cell and now she realized it was the cord she needed.

"So I'm guessing you've been busy catching up with old friends."

Her grip tightened around the cord. "I told you before that I came here for Mimi. Well, Jane, actually. But as it turns out, Ellen MacBride, who was like a second mother to me, is in the hospital, so I'm really glad I came."

"Hmmm, I see. That would be Daniel's mother, right? So how did Daniel react to seeing you again?"

"For chrissake, stop it. Please!" She took a breath and lowered her voice. "I called because I miss you."

He was quiet for a moment. "Okay. I miss you too, Mel." She heard him inhaling. "How is your aunt?"

"She's holding on. Nasty as ever."

"Have you decided ...?"

"I'm sitting with it like you suggested."

"Right."

Her head was reeling with all the stuff she knew she shouldn't tell him, so it was hard to know what to talk about next.

"Anyway, the big news in town is that a woman I went to school with, Sally Walters, is missing." She paused. "I'm thinking it might have the makings of a book. I don't mean that to sound cavalier. I feel really awful about it. The truth is she was a bit of a slut and I never liked her much, so that sort of makes me feel worse, you know? I'm following the story and hoping she comes out of it okay."

"Isn't Daniel the chief of police there now?"

"Yes."

Stephen was quiet for a few seconds. There was no reason to say anything more; they both knew what he was thinking.

"So when do you think you'll be coming home?"

"I don't know yet."

Silence again.

"Well, let me know when you do. Goodbye, Melissa."

She straightened out the cord and replaced the phone in the cradle on the wall.

Stephen closed his cell phone, but held on to it for a few minutes before placing it in the holster on his belt. He knew Melissa better than she thought, maybe better than she knew herself. And it sounded like better than even odds that this poor girl was dead. Melissa would be knee-deep in the investigation and help Daniel solve the case. Hell, they'd probably never seen a murder in that town. With her analytical reporter skills, she'd figure it out. Then she and Daniel would live happily ever after. That's what she'd always wanted, even if she didn't know it yet. He did. He rubbed his forehead in irritation.

Christ, how he wanted to jump in his car and drive there, physically put her in his car, and bring her home. The thought brought a grim smile to his face, which faded fast. *Like that would work.* Damn, maybe that crap Tiff was talking at dinner the other night made sense which was totally annoying. He would have to wait. He had spent the last few nights coming to terms with the fact that she might not come back. The thought devastated him, but the next move had to be hers.

Melissa had run upstairs and stretched out on her bed. She closed her eyes, deep in thought. She was startled when her cell phone rang. She picked it up from the nightstand and looked at the caller ID. *Madison.*

"Hi cuz. How are you?"

"I'm great, Melissa, but the question should be—how are you? I hope you don't mind but I called the apartment and Stephen filled me in on your trip. He said he thought maybe you could use someone to talk to. How's it going?"

"I feel like I'm just hanging around here waiting ... I don't know if Magee told you that my Aunt Mimi has cancer. It's just a matter of time."

"I'm really sorry to hear that, but as I recall she wasn't your favorite person."

"That's an understatement. But Aunt Jane called and asked me to come. I came because she asked, but I'm getting the distinct feeling that Mimi wishes I would leave."

"Oh, Mel, I'm sure she's happy to see you and spend some time with you before ... before it's too late.

"I know you're right, but I swore I'd never come back and here I am. I feel like a hypocrite in so many ways. I've spent most of my adult life despising her, and doing everything I could think of to humiliate her and now ..."

"None of that seems to matter anymore." Madison said softly.

"Right. It's like I'm finally realizing that I spent so much time and energy hating her that I wasted precious time of my own. I guess watching someone die makes us think about how we live our lives. Wow, I'm really philosophical today."

"And you're right, sweetie. Listen, I'm only about two hours away and I'll come if you need me. I hope you know that."

"Thanks, Maddie, but I'm okay. I may actually go home for a few days to get some clothes and then come back in. I'll let you know for sure."

"Okay, I've got to run. I'm volunteering at the hospital this morning but I wanted to let you know I'm thinking about you. Love you, cuz. Take care and keep in touch.

"Bye, Maddie, love you too."

Melissa dialed Stephen.

"Thanks so much, Stephen. It was good to talk to Maddie. She's so grounded and always has the ability to calm me."

"I'm just glad she called when she did. I felt like you needed someone to talk to who isn't emotionally involved."

This was it, his opening. Stephen searched his memory for the words he had prepared but thought he might never get a chance to say.

"I'm happy that you found your cousins when you did and that they will be there for you no matter what happens. I want you to have someone to talk to who understands what you have gone through and who you are." He inhaled and forced himself to keep going. There was no turning back now.

"We're more alike than you know, Mel. Behind the intellect and the confidence, there's that wall of defense no one gets past. People can feel it in us even if they don't know what to do about it. My family loves me but they find me confusing and don't always understand me."

Stephen continued. "Do you remember back in the hospital when you guessed about my family and how I didn't fit into it at first? Well, you couldn't have been more right. My rough-and-tumble working class Irish family was presented with a shy bookworm who got beat up in school. My brothers, hell even my sister, had to keep an eye on me all the time. I had that come-punch-me face. And you were salvaged by Jane and then Ellen but without the family you should have had. So we have inside us this secret center that we protect at all costs so we can survive if we wind up alone." He felt his cheeks burning; it wasn't coming out right at all.

"I don't think it really has to be that way. I won't believe it, not anymore." He hurried on, afraid she'd stop listening. "And now you have your cousins, who share more than just your middle name. They will always be there for you."

Melissa was astonished at this thoughtful, long speech and choked up by the end of it.

"Thank you, Stephen, I can't tell you how much that means to me."

"You don't have to. I just hope you realize what you mean to me." He took a breath. "So, no matter what happens, you won't be alone."

"Stephen ..."

"It's all right. I love you, Mel." He clicked off, sparing her the need to reply.

She flashed back to the hospital when they'd met the first time. She didn't believe now that she really wanted to commit suicide. She was just so tired and so cold. The cold was killing her. It started with being unable to laugh and ended with a numbing chill that made her blood thicken day by day. Her secret center was freezing, numbing cold.

She shook it off and went to find her aunts. She brought Jane into Mimi's room so she could tell them both. It was time they knew. Mimi sat up straighter and took in the bright smile on Melissa's face.

"I have something to tell you both that may surprise you. I know that your parents for whatever reason cut all ties with family years ago—generations ago for that matter. But a few years back, while doing some genealogy research, I found that I have two cousins who are both about my age. When we got together to meet in person, we discovered that each of us has the "gift". We had always assumed we were alone but now we know we aren't."

Jane and Mimi exchanged glances.

Jane spoke first. "Well, my goodness. Isn't that ... wonderful?" Her hand flew to her chest as it always did when she was flustered.

"Why, Mimi, I believe I did hear years ago that Aunt Melinda had a daughter and one of these girls must be her grandchild. But I'm afraid I don't know who the other is, would you have any idea?"

Melissa watched Mimi closely as she seemed to compose herself after the initial shock of this news.

"No, I would have no idea. I've never had the slightest interest in seeking out distant relatives. As you said, we lost touch years ago." Mimi closed her eyes for a second. "So you say there are two."

"Yes, Magee is married and lives in Connecticut and she has a young son. She was a paralegal but is now getting her law degree in family law with the main focus on child advocacy.

"Madison lives in Lancaster where she is an organic farmer. She has two boys and actually grew up not far from here. She and her husband met while studying horticulture at Penn State."

"So you're not the only one. That's how it's supposed to be," her aunt murmured. To both Jane and Melissa's surprise, a look of relief spread over the gaunt face. She sighed and seemed to doze off, eyes closed, breathing quietly.

Jane patted Melissa's arm and they walked downstairs together. Jane prepared sandwiches for lunch and added homemade cookies to each plate. They sat at the kitchen table and chatted while they ate. Jane went to tend her garden. It was a beautiful day outside and Melissa had a lot to think about so she decided to take a long walk around town.

CHAPTER TWENTY-EIGHT

Sylvan Mills was built on seven hills, just like Rome, a standard joke with the locals. The steep slopes were compacted tightly within a square mile and a couple of them rose almost as sharply as those in San Francisco. Melissa left the house just after noon and headed toward the edge of town.

As she hiked up Allegheny Street where it intersected Bishop, she caught a flash of dog out of the corner of her eye. She looked down the hill and saw a golden retriever, not running flat out, but loping happily along in a familiar way.

"Lily!" she called. Sure enough, the dog turned, gave her that ever-present retriever grin, and then kept on going.

Melissa now wished she had changed to her running shoes. The flat-soled sandals she was wearing were very comfortable for walking, but not too practical for chasing after a dog. But she was certain Lily was not supposed to be running loose. She finally caught up with her as she ambled along the railroad tracks that went past the dump. "Lily, Lily, come back here."

The dog had stopped to investigate a pile of black trash bags at the edge of the dump. She looked up at the sound of her name but then went back to her digging, tail flagging cheerfully.

"Lily, it's me."

The dog gave her a quick once over but the trash seemed more interesting. She flicked her tongue across her lips and went back to ripping at the bags.

"Come on, Lily. Come on, girl. You're in enough trouble." She came up beside the dog. "Come on. I mean it.

This is gross." She caught a whiff. "Oooh, you're so gonna need a bath."

Melissa looked around but there was no sign of help on the way. She reached down to grab hold of the dog's collar. As she pulled back, the black plastic bag Lily wouldn't let go of broke wide open. When Melissa saw it, and smelled it, a wave of nausea rushed up her throat and kept her from screaming.

At the same moment, a dirty black pickup truck pulled up fast and jerked to a stop. The driver jumped out and came toward Melissa, his face unfriendly. When Sam saw the torn bag, he stopped cold.

Daniel's radio had gone off a few minutes earlier. "Hey, chief, your dog's loose again."

"Sonofabitch." He threw the Jeep into third gear and raced out toward the dump. The only good thing about Lily getting out was that, once she got over the thrill of being free, the old dog always went to the same place.

When Daniel saw Sam standing next to Melissa, his heart went to his knees. He slammed the vehicle to a stop, jumped out and ran through the gate. Melissa had Lily by the collar, and her face was white, with a distinct greenish tinge. She saw him coming and waved frantically with her free hand.

"Daniel over here. Oh, Lord. Oh, Lord." She pointed toward a piece of black plastic sticking out of the trash piles and he headed toward it. Melissa took Lily to the Jeep and put her in the back before bending over and being sick in the grass. *Poor Sally! It had to be.*

It was all Daniel could do to keep from doing the same when he bent down and saw strands of long blonde hair. He straightened up and looked at the man standing silently beside him.

Melissa took deep breaths, willing herself not to give in to the dry heaves. As a reporter in the city, she had been the first to get to a crime scene or two. But it was the first time she'd ever been this close to a less-than-fresh body covered with maggots. She gulped for air.

Daniel glanced toward her then strode over to the Jeep and pulled a bottle of water from under the front seat. "Think about something else." He tossed her the bottle and pulled out his radio.

She shook her head to clear it of the image of the bag and poor Sally, what was left of her. She concentrated on breathing and on happy images: blue skies, ocean waves, white clouds.

A squad car came screeching to a halt, lights flashing. Red Dixon was out of the car almost before it stopped. He and Daniel exchanged a few short sentences as Red kept glancing toward the trash pile. Daniel kept a hand on Red's arm and shook his head. He told Red to take Melissa home. She decided this was no time to argue and she badly needed to lie down. Red was blessedly silent during the short ride. Melissa knew she should give him some word of comfort but she was, for once, speechless with shock.

By three o'clock, Daniel was briefing his entire force of eight men. "Okay, guys, listen up. We have a murder on our hands. The state police will be helping us out. I don't want to hear that any of you are spreading rumors until we get some facts. Of course, we can expect the ... remains ... to be identified as Sally Walters, seeing as how she's the only one missing around here. We've already had Sam in for questioning but I don't think it's gonna stick. So Sam's gonna be out there as usual. He's got a temper and Melissa Sullivan's crossed him so we can't afford to take our eye off that ball either. I want all patrol cars going past the Witherspoon house on a regular basis and make sure Sam sees you around the dump and his house, too." He cleared his throat. "Of course, finding out who did this to Sally will be our number one priority. Keep your ears to the ground." He paused and cleared his throat. "We all knew Sally. She didn't deserve this. We've gotta get this guy."

CHAPTER TWENTY-NINE

At that same moment, Sam was collapsing into a chair behind a cluttered desk in the grimy construction trailer that served as his office. *Sweet Mother of God.*

He put his hands over his face and planted his elbows on his desk. He and Lou had kicked back a few out at the cabin a couple nights ago and Lou had let it slip that Max told him Sally was knocked up by some big shot and there was going to be hell to pay. Sam figured they'd pay her off and send her out of town to take care of it. It had been done before. But he had never imagined this. He took a solid swig out of the whiskey bottle he kept in his bottom drawer. The warmth of the golden liquid felt good going down but not when it started back up. He raced for the bathroom. After washing up, he sat down heavily in his chair.

There weren't that many assholes in this town and even fewer who had the balls to leave her in his dump. He felt sick again. Max, the crazy bastard, probably thought it was funny dumping Sally in the trash.

Sam knew MacBride would be hauling him back in for more questioning once the dust settled. He swallowed hard. Who was gonna believe that he hadn't done it? *Only Jillie.* He picked up the phone but then put it back down and stood up; he had to tell her to her face, before somebody else did.

CHAPTER THIRTY

Jane was waiting for Melissa with a cup of chamomile tea. "Police scanner," she said. "Everybody in town's got one." Melissa told her aunt she had been there.

"It's a damned shame." Jane commented. "Some folks just seem to be born with no chance at all." She told Melissa she was going to work in the garden, her own way of dealing with the blues, she said with a sad smile.

Melissa went upstairs and peeked into Mimi's room. She seemed to be sleeping. Bad news would keep, she decided. Her aunt looked so fragile laying there, Melissa felt oddly moved. Death up close had softened her up, maybe. But the Witherspoon voice in her head said that it was time for her to act. She tiptoed into the room.

She recited a prayer for protection in her head. She shakily approached her aunt's side. Just as her hand touched Mimi's wrist, her aunt stirred. Melissa held her breath but kept her fingertips on the cool skin. She closed her eyes and was about to open herself up to Mimi's condition when she heard a sharp, "No!"

Melissa gasped. Mimi softened her tone. "No, Melissa." Mimi gently removed Melissa's hand. "Save your strength for those who deserve it. I won't have it."

In response to the hurt look on Melissa's face, she added, "Go, child. It's all right ... but ... thank you." Melissa was as surprised as her aunt by the tears that splashed down her cheeks. Perhaps it was the mist from her own but she could have sworn she saw tears in Mimi's eyes, too.

Melissa stumbled down the stairs as the doorbell rang. She brushed the tears away and hurried to answer it before it disturbed Mimi, throwing open the door to find Tom MacBride just stepping off the porch.

Melissa lightened up as fast as she could. "Hey, Tom. Sorry. I was upstairs and didn't hear the doorbell ringing."

"No problem." Reacting to the look on her face as well as the shadows under her eyes, he said, "Well, maybe I'll come by another time."

She forced a smile. "Don't be silly. Come on in."

He stepped into the hallway, looking around cautiously.

"Mimi's upstairs in her room."

He relaxed and smiled at her. "Well, okay. Anyway my wife asked me to see if you'd like to come out for a visit and some lunch tomorrow. I know it's been a lousy day but what do you think?"

"Lunch, tomorrow?" Melissa repeated still a little confused by what had just happened upstairs.

Jane came down the hallway, peeling off her gardening gloves. "Hi, Tom. Good to see you. How are Annie and that adorable little fellow of yours?"

"Good, good. I was, uh, just seeing if Melissa wanted to have lunch with us tomorrow."

Jane put an arm around Melissa's waist. "Of course she does. That's a great idea."

Melissa exhaled. "Okay, sure. It sounds great."

"I'll pick you up tomorrow around 11:30 if that's okay. Annie will be happy to see you again."

"Sounds perfect. I'll be ready."

After Tom went down the steps, Melissa turned to Jane. She told her she had tried to help Mimi. Jane wiped her eyes on her apron. "Why am I not surprised? Has to do everything the hard way, doesn't she?" She gave Melissa a hug.

"Well, we've done all we can and that's what matters. Someday, Melissa, that will be important to you." She composed herself.

"I'm gonna go lie down for awhile, I think I've had all the excitement I can stand for one day. See you later, Aunt Jane."

CHAPTER THIRTY-ONE

Annie MacBride moved the baby to her hip and hugged Melissa with her free arm. Melissa reached for Tommy, who drooled happily down his bib as she cooed at him.

"Obviously, he's feeling better. But now he's cutting teeth," Annie said, wiping his face.

The baby grabbed Melissa's hair and started to chew on it. She pulled it back and then he took an interest in her gold hoop earrings. His mother shook her head and took him back.

Lily came bounding with great leaps from the back of the mobile home.

"So this is where you get sent when you misbehave." Melissa bent down and scratched behind the golden ears.

"We don't mind. It's probably easier for Daniel and Ellen, until she's back on her feet, anyway." Annie settled Tommy into his highchair and pulled it next to hers at the kitchen table. "Thanks for coming, Melissa. It's a rare treat for me to have an adult to talk to these days, especially a woman. Tom works so hard, between the construction business and the band, and then he's a volunteer fireman as well. When he does have any down time, he's working on Daniel's house. Most of my girlfriends work, too, so I don't get much company out here."

"It must be lonely for you. But I guess it's worth it." She looked at the baby, spitting baby food back out at his mother as fast as she could spoon it in, and hearing "Daniel's house" echo in her head.

Annie laughed. "Yes, it is, incredible as that may seem. I'm married to the man I love and I have this little character to keep me busy." Tom strolled back into the kitchen as if on cue. "Ready for lunch, honey?"

He gave her a quick hug and settled at the table to feed Tommy while Annie served the meal. Melissa was astonished to find that lunch consisted of a salad, beef stew, and big, thick slices of homemade bread. When the large cherry pie followed, Melissa crossed her eyes and Tom laughed until he choked.

Annie explained. "Half the time, Tom doesn't make it home for dinner. So I try to get him a decent meal whenever I can."

Daniel walked in just as Melissa was refilling their coffee mugs to go with the pie, while Annie tied a clean bib around the baby's chubby neck.

"Too late for lunch, but at least I made it in time for dessert." He pulled up a chair.

Annie, taking the hint, offered him a plate of hot stew out of the pot, which he accepted with a grateful nod.

"You look beat, Daniel," Annie commented. She lowered her voice as if the baby would hear and understand her. "We heard about Sally."

His head stayed bent over his plate. "Yeah, I've been at it all night but we've got everybody on board. It's just a matter of time now." He reached for a mug and met Melissa's eyes, then turned to Tom. "Work on the house this afternoon?"

"Sure, if you're up to it."

He shrugged. "I think a couple of hours out of the office might help clear my head. I'll go check back in before I try to get some sleep."

"Okay, but I have to run Melissa back into town. I picked her up and brought her out for lunch."

Annie spoke up. "Hey, why don't we all go take a look at the house? I haven't seen it since you started the interior. I'd love to see it, wouldn't you, Melissa? Maybe you could ride back in with Daniel later."

Melissa hesitated. "Sure."

Daniel drained his coffee. "Okay. I guess that works."

Melissa forced a smile. "I can't wait to see it. Where is it anyway?"

Annie smiled brightly. "Remember the hill Daniel's grandfather left to him? The view's gorgeous."

Melissa ran a hand through her hair, hooking the white section behind her right ear. "Of course, Kerin's Hill."

The women took the baby in Annie's small sedan and Tom and Daniel followed in the Jeep. When they had all gotten out of their vehicles, Melissa stood staring at the two-story house on the crest, surrounded by construction debris and equipment. Tom moved to his wife's side and spoke to her in a low voice. They remained by the car playing with the baby as Melissa moved inside.

Melissa walked through the house while Daniel trailed silently behind her. There were windows everywhere, some of them diamond-paned, turning the sunlight into dancing patterns on the gleaming wood floors. It was beautifully simple and clean, light and roomy, without pretension. She found herself drawn back to the bay window in the kitchen with its stunning view of the mountains with their halo of clouds, the valley in the sunlight, and the wildflowers on the hill.

It brought tears to her eyes. "Oh, my."

Daniel's deep voice came from just behind her. "I told you I was going to build it."

"I remember."

She turned to face him and he could see in her eyes the effects of light and space and tears.

"So here we are." His tired face forced itself into some semblance of a smile. "What do you think?"

Melissa relented. "It's absolutely perfect. It's amazing. It suits you."

He smiled back. "Thanks." He paused. "I started building it long before I got engaged. It's my house."

She felt like he was trying to read her mind and turned back to look out the window. Tom was tossing his son into the air under Annie's watchful eye. She decided a change in subject was in order. "So there's nothing on Sally yet?"

He frowned. "So far the last person who admits to having seen her is Red Dixon."

"No way, I remember when he was little and used to follow us around. It can't be him."

"I don't think so." He hesitated. "He told me what happened and his story seems credible."

She waited him out; finally he repeated Red's story ...

Sally was barreling up the hill in her little car, heading out of town, when she heard the short blast of the siren. She looked in her rearview. "Oh, crap."

Red tapped on the passenger window. "Let me in, Sally." He jumped in to get out of the rain. "Sally, Sally, you never learn, do ya? This is the second time this week."

She smiled big and flashed her green eyes at him. "Come on, Red, cut me a break. I'm late for an appointment."

"Darlin', you were born late. You've gotten way too many breaks already and you know it. It's your license this time."

Her smile faded. "You're kiddin', right?"

"Nope. I just ran it. You're gonna be lucky to get off with six months and driving school, Sal. You're over the limit."

She turned in her seat and leaned over the gearshift with her low-cut pink top and pouty hot pink lips. "Look, Red, maybe we can work this out. Ya know, just between us?"

"How'd you figure?"

"I'm thinkin' maybe we could get together. What do you say?"

He considered for a few seconds, snapped his book shut, and then looked at her. "My place? Tonight?"

The smile returned. "You got it. I can't make it 'til after ten but I'll be there. Gotta go, baby."

He leaned across the car, his face close to hers. "Don't disappoint me, Sally. And keep your goddamned foot off the floorboard."

She ran a sharp fingernail down the side of his cheek and said, "See ya later, lover."

"And that's how it happened. He said he waited with the porch light on until midnight, then turned it off and went to bed."

"She never came?"

He shook his head. "Poor kid. He said he figured he was the only guy in town who hadn't ... well, he's never done anything like that before."

"Any idea on the cause of death?"

"The state police medical examiner says strangulation. That's confidential, of course."

"Of course." She nodded but there were alarm bells going off in her head. He said that far too casually, considering it was his only lead in a murder investigation. She hoped it was inexperience. Melissa felt that old familiar queasiness in the pit of her stomach. Daniel had never been very subtle, even as a teenager. Was he expecting a quid pro quo here?

When she'd found the CD in Sally's room, tucked into a music case of The Flys, "Got You Where I Want You", Melissa had been overcome by the urge to hide it under her shirt. So Johnny didn't know she had it; Daniel couldn't know. She had read it straight through with the lyric of that song playing in the background, every other chorus ending in, "I'm dying here." Sally could have had no idea it would be so hauntingly apropos.

As soon as Melissa had read a few pages, she had made the decision that only if something had happened to Sally, *and* if a suspect came up *and* if the connection was made, would she consider giving it up.

He was watching her and it was time to change the subject. "Daniel ... the other day ..."

"Why did I take off and leave you like that?"

She nodded.

He paused and gave her an answer he had clearly given a lot of thought. "It just hit me that I had betrayed Jennifer. She's going to be my wife and deserves my loyalty and respect. It shouldn't have been so ... easy ... for me to forget that."

"I see."

He knew she didn't, not really. "What about your guy? How do you think he'd react?"

Melissa was startled. "Stephen?" She thought about it. "I think he'd want me to ... be sure I knew what I wanted before I married him or anybody, for that matter."

Daniel raised his eyebrows. "He's a better man than I am, then. Does that mean you're going to tell him?"

"Probably, eventually." She gave him a quick smile. "I'm a Witherspoon. I have enough secrets. Are you going to tell Jennifer?"

"Hell, no. And I hope to God she never finds out."

The silence stood between them until Daniel turned to leave and Melissa followed him silently out to where a subdued Annie was waiting.

"Don't you want to see the house, Annie?"

"Oh, I'll see it another time. Maybe we should go."

Melissa smiled absently down at her and reached for the baby. "Let's do that."

Daniel and Tom stripped off their shirts and went to work on the crown molding. Tom kept looking over at Daniel but said nothing. After an hour or so, they stopped for a drink of water.

Daniel wiped his face and said, "Stop it."

Tom looked at him. "What?"

"Not saying whatever you're thinking over there."

"Hey, pal, it's your life. But if you want me to say it." He laid a hand on Daniel's shoulder. "I think you're making the biggest mistake of your life. You were just kids when you let her get away the first time, but letting her walk again ..." He shook his head and picked up a hammer. Daniel wanted to tell Tom that he simply didn't understand but said nothing. Tom would never get it, just like his mom didn't get it.

They knocked off around suppertime and drove back to Tom's mobile home.

Melissa hopped into the Jeep with Daniel, waving to the baby as Annie helped him wave from the window. They drove back into town, exchanging the briefest of comments on houses they passed or people they knew, both feeling awkward, emotionally and physically exhausted.

As he pulled up to the house, Daniel spoke again. "Melissa, I want to be sure you understand. You left and didn't come back ..." He forestalled her speaking by raising a hand, "I know, because of Mimi, but you didn't come back for me either. Your hatred of her was stronger than your feelings for me."

Melissa's mouth opened but nothing came out. He stared her down. His tone was bitter, "It took me years to understand that and get over it, please don't ask me to start all over again."

When Mimi called to her as she passed by the living room, Melissa forced past the lump in her throat and threw some excuse back over her shoulder. She couldn't bear to see Mimi gloat over the embarrassed flush on her face. "Uh, I'm really sorry, Mimi, but I have a dinner date with Howard and Donna tonight. I'll be around most of the day tomorrow, I promise."

CHAPTER THIRTY-TWO

After a rather subdued dinner at Donna's, Melissa found herself walking past her own house and continuing around the block. She meandered down into town again. Her thoughts tumbled over each other, mostly questions with no answers. *What did she want? Which life was really meant to be hers?* A shuffling sound broke the stillness of the darkened street. Melissa looked around, aware now that she was in the middle of a deserted little town that, except for the bars, rolled up its sidewalks around six. This was not good.

She turned abruptly and started walking at a rapid clip back toward Witherspoon Lane. The hair on the back of her neck stood up. Noises behind her ... a truck door opening ... heavy footsteps. Fight or run?

In split second, Melissa took off full speed toward the only light she could see. The town gas station/quickie mart was one of the few places that stayed open late in Sylvan Mills. As she threw open the door, panting, the teenager sitting behind the cash register reading a magazine looked up and his mouth flew open. She caught her breath. "Hi, I'm Melissa Sullivan."

"Shoot, no need to tell me that. Everybody in town knows who you are." He grinned showing a glimpse of chewing tobacco inside his lower lip.

She caught her breath and gave him her best smile in return. "Well, I sort of managed to get lost and I could use a ride home."

"Sure, no problem." He grabbed his keys and headed out the door, setting the little clock sign to "back in ten minutes." She waited inside until he had the lights on, then moved quickly and jumped into the battered up old pickup.

She chattered politely during the short ride while her eyes were glued to the side mirror. When they pulled up in front, she hesitated.

"You want me to walk you to the door, ma'am?"

His concerned face touched her. "No, I'm ... good. I can't thank you enough, uh."

"Pete, my name's Pete, Pete Moran. Well, if you could sign one of them books for my mom, it would be cool."

Even distracted, it made her laugh. "No problem, I'll drop it by the store tomorrow. Thanks, Pete." She jumped out and sprinted up the walk and steps, then turned to wave at the boy still watching at the curb. He waved back and took off.

It was only when her head hit the pillow that Melissa started to shake uncontrollably. She thought about calling Daniel, but he had warned her, hadn't he? She was stupid not to realize that Sam would try to get even. She hadn't actually seen his face but she didn't have to.

CHAPTER THIRTY-THREE

Jill had made her bed and, as her mother constantly reminded her, she would have to lie in it. God knew she tried to make the best of it, even when he came home drunk and she thought for sure he was going to kill her. But maybe Melissa wasn't completely wrong. Maybe she should be stronger. For the first time ever, she was listening in on his phone conversation. She was frightened and furious, afraid to breathe, her ear pressed against the extension in the bedroom.

"Hey, buddy. That Sullivan broad turned out to be pretty slippery."

"And you weren't much help, so you still owe me."

Max was dangerously quiet.

Sam glanced toward the bedroom and lowered his voice. "Don't forget I know it was you threw Sally's body in my dump to set me up, you bastard. Or did you just think that was funny?"

Max laughed. "Ashes to ashes, trash to trash." Max forestalled the tirade that was coming. "Listen, I told you before, no need to panic. There's no way they can pin anything on you. Even you wouldn't be dumb enough to throw her in your own dump, think about it. But I can still help you out with the Sullivan bitch, if you're ready to get serious this time?"

Jill cradled the phone against her cheek.

"Now you're talkin'," Sam said eagerly.

There was a moment of silence, followed by a loud sigh. "But nothing permanent, man, I got enough problems. You hear me? We just want to teach her a lesson and run her ass out of town."

"That works for me. Meet me tomorrow night around ten down at the dump. I'll have something for you."

Jill wept silently, one hand clutching the gold cross around her neck.

"Right."

He hung up fast and she put down the phone and dashed back to bed, turning on her side to hide her frantic face as he opened the bedroom door.

Max redialed and Garrett Anniston quietly picked up the phone in his library.

"Hey, it's me. We need to talk. I think I got an answer to your, uh, pest problem."

Anniston answered, "You will be careful, Max. This is simply a ... pest removal ... not an extermination."

Max chuckled. "Leave it to me."

After that call, the man on the other end sat in his big leather chair, smoked a pipe, and considered the options. Finally, he dialed another number. "We have a situation."

Mimi was glad she had gotten to the phone before Jane. She answered in a whisper, "Are you insane, calling me when she's here?"

She could almost see his condescending smile on the other end of the line. "Well, I don't have much choice these days. Or would you rather I come over?"

"Listen to me," she hissed. "You come anywhere near her and I'll ..."

"Again with the threats," He sighed heavily. "I'm simply calling you as a courtesy. If you don't want to see the girl get hurt, get her out of town, now!" He paused. "I can't control everyone, you know."

"Her name is Melissa, just like mine. It's not hard to remember. And I'm dying as fast as I can." She wanted to slam the receiver down, then caught herself and replaced it quietly. Her vision blurred. Who would protect Melissa when she was gone?

Mimi tucked the blanket under her feet. Perhaps tomorrow she would talk to Melissa, tell her to go home. If she had to make her hate her more than she did now, that was all right, too. She was not safe here. God willing, some day she would understand. She sighed and closed her eyes against the latest wave of pain. *Lord, please just let it be over.*

She had tried to save them all. She had fought the old man in a way that would have made him proud if the target had been someone else. When she caught him looking at Jane *that* way, she had marched into his study and closed the door. She laid it all down for him. Video, photos, tapes—several copies carefully stashed. He laughed and said she was bluffing. He stopped laughing when she pulled the mini recorder out of her pocket.

Jane followed her dreams to Chicago. Emily married Rob. If either of them had any idea the price their older sister had paid, it was not discussed. When the old man, drunk on his ass, ran his car straight into a tree out by the state park, Mimi made a call and the sheriff called it an accident.

Mimi couldn't see how she deserved heaven. But she found it hard to believe that any deity would send her to hell where the old man was surely waiting.

CHAPTER THIRTY-FOUR

It was time to ramp it up. Daniel intended to spend his day talking to everyone who had contact with Sally in the few days prior to her death. He drove to the hospital gift shop to start with Donna. He knew his locals and his women well enough to know that asking her to come to the station would destroy her concentration and limit any useful information she might be able to give him.

He walked casually up to the gift shop counter. "Hey, Donna."

She looked up from the box of stuffed animals and laid down her pricing gun. "Hi, Daniel. You're here about Sally, aren't you?"

He smiled what he hoped was a reassuring smile. "Well, she wasn't close to that many people, Donna, so you're my best chance to get some insight into what was going on with her." He leaned forward confidentially. "I know I can count on you to tell me anything she might have said that would help find her ... *killer*." He emphasized the word; Donna lived for drama.

Donna's eyes widened. "Sure."

"Great. So can you give me any idea who Sally was dating in the last few weeks?"

A woman approached the counter with a balloon and a card. Donna rang up her purchases and then turned back to Daniel.

"You know, I have tried to think about it. She never wanted to say his name; it was like she didn't want to jinx it. She just called him the man of her dreams. But you know Sally, she can't really keep a secret. So I pretty much figured out it was someone who was working at the courthouse." She swallowed. "There's a new ADA over there who's pretty cute. I never asked her because I thought she just get, you know, pissed off that I'd guessed."

"Thanks. That's a big help."

Donna brightened. "And, I guess I should mention ..."

Daniel was writing in a small notepad he had pulled from his shirt pocket.

"Well, I don't want to point fingers? But one day we were at O'Malley's and that Sylvan State quarterback, Rick Jones, was in a booth with his guys. Sally was like telling me about how he took her to a Black-Eyed Peas Concert back in high school and then she sort ... implied ... that he was, well disappointing, shall we say, had some ... shortcomings. When he saw her giggling, his face turned real red and ugly. He looked so mad! Can you believe he still isn't over it? I told her to, like, shut up and we got out of there." Daniel made a note.

Donna twirled a strand of red hair around her finger. "And, I was sure you knew that before she was seeing this last guy, she was like hanging out with ... Jeff Carpellino?"

Daniel's face twitched. Donna's habit of making every sentence sound like a question when she was nervous was endearing most days but not today.

"Well, of course, he's married to Maria Tessi, whose family owns every restaurant in the county, and who rumor has it, has connections, if you know what I mean? He just talked Maria into buying him that 'vette that's been sitting on Confer's lot forever and they have those three little kids, so I was thinking that if Sally got ... knocked up, that would really piss him off, you know?"

The color had drained from Daniel's face. "And I thought I should, maybe, mention that the last night she worked, as I was leaving, that Max guy came in? The wierd one who went to like the Gulf War and never really came back. Yeah, the guy who walks around town in camos and carries a shotgun in his truck like all year 'round, even when it's not hunting season? Well, he was, uh, sniffing around and Sally told him to get the hell away from her and stay away in a really loud voice. I mean like, geez, she had some standards, if you know what I mean. What a creep!"

Another customer entered the shop. Donna took a deep breath. "Okay, that's it." She turned back to her box and then stopped Daniel as he was leaving. "Oh wait. I want to make sure somebody mentioned to you that Sally had been hanging out at the truck stop out by I80 on Saturday nights? They have a band, you know? There's some pretty cute truckers going by there. Of course, there's some creepy guys, too. I know for a fact that she hasn't gone since she started dating this new guy she was all fired up about but if she got knocked up, say, like a couple of months ago, well, it might have been ... I saw this TV movie once about a serial killer truck driver." Donna paused for breath. "Wow, I feel much better." She said cheerfully. She turned to wait on the customer.

Daniel walked slowly out to his Jeep and sank into the driver's seat. He lowered his head until it was resting against the steering wheel.

CHAPTER THIRTY-FIVE

By noon, Daniel had dutifully found out that the ex-football player had moved out of state and the unfaithful husband was a wimpy little cuss who didn't seem tough enough to strangle anybody. Max Vinterra kept rising up the charts. Daniel had no problem calling him into the office; Max was unlikely to be intimidated by police.

He sauntered in and slouched into the seat opposite Daniel's desk.

"Thanks for coming in."

"No problem, man." He raised his hands in a gesture of innocence. "I got nothin' to hide. Damn shame, what happened to that poor girl."

Daniel swallowed his distaste and kept his face impassive. "Yes, it was. Can you tell me how well you knew her?"

Max's eyes narrowed. "Well, I ain't gonna deny that I might have had a go once in a while. Hell, everybody else did. But we wasn't engaged or nothin' if that's what you mean."

"Would you mind telling me where you were last Saturday night, Max?"

The man straightened up. "You accusin' me here? 'Cause I can get me a lawyer."

"Easy now." Daniel said soothingly. "I'm just doing my job. I have to ask the same questions of everyone who knew Sally."

That brought an ugly grin to his unshaven face. "Must be haulin' em in by the busload."

Daniel forced a smile in return. "It hasn't been easy."

"Okay, chief. I was playin' poker with Lou and some boys over to his basement there on Wilson Street all night.

Went through damn near three cases of beer." He shook his head sadly. "Lost about fifty bucks."

"And Sunday?"

"Spent most of the mornin' sleepin' it off. Then I was over to my sister's for Sunday dinner. Watched some football. That's about it."

Daniel wrote it all down and then stood up. "Reckon you'll have no trouble signing a statement on that for me, right?"

Max's eyes narrowed. "Everybody doin' that?"

Daniel looked him squarely in the eyes. "Nope."

"Guess I'll take a pass then. 'Less we git my lawyer to look it over first."

Daniel nodded.

The man left, head high, clearly pleased with himself.

This didn't surprise Daniel. It also didn't surprise him that Max would use his cousin and his sister as alibis. He could have sworn the moon was blue and they would have backed him up. Max stayed number one on Daniel's list. Now the question was whether he had killed Sally on his own or done it for somebody else. The list of people Max Vinterra might do such things for was a short one.

It was turning into a long day. He still had the Courthouse to check out.

CHAPTER THIRTY-SIX

First thing in the morning, Garrett Anniston walked into Brian's office. He noted the pallor of his young colleague's face. He wondered if this kid was cut out for politics at all.

"How are you doing?" He asked politely.

"Okay, I guess."

The impeccably dressed Anniston leaned towards the smaller man. "Have you been in touch with the police chief?"

"What?"

He sighed. "I cannot continue to do all of your thinking for you, Jackson. He's already started working his way through everyone who knew the girl, he will find you. "

"Ah, Christ, I thought you were going to protect me." He swallowed. "I didn't do anything."

Garrett smiled benignly. "I said I would help you and I will. But some effort is going to be required on your part. You need to be front and center, grieving and concerned with finding Sally's killer."

"I don't know ..."

"You listen to me, boy. It's time to man up. You take your balls firmly in hand and you be seen all over this town mourning your fiancé or you pack your bags and run. Of course, that might just make you look guilty as hell. I'd hate to see that happen." But his shrug said "so be it."

It was as if he could actually see the light bulb above the kid's head.

Giving him credit, once he got it, he got it. Brian picked up the phone and called the only funeral home in town to make sure arrangements were being made. They weren't. He asked about her father but was given Donna's number. She was much moved and said she'd get word to Johnny who had no phone. He offered up his credit card for whatever she needed to do. He almost ran to his car and drove himself to the police station.

When Daniel opened the door to his office after Max left, he was waiting outside.

After ushering him in politely, Daniel asked, "What can I do for you, sir?"

The young man, who stood in front of him all atremble with intense emotion, cleared his throat and wiped his eyes. "I'm Brian Jackson. I've been working at the courthouse for a couple of months as an ADA. I came to see you, chief, to see if you've found Sally's killer." He sniffed and looked Daniel in the eye. "We were going to be married, you know."

Daniel exhaled loudly. "No, Mr. Jackson, I didn't know that. Maybe you'd better take a seat."

Half an hour later, Brian had woven a moving tale of how he was new in the area and didn't know anyone and how Sally had befriended him. He admitted with a red face that they had kept their relationship quiet because of his political aspirations. They figured once they were married, her background would be forgotten. How he couldn't bear the thought of someone harming his precious girl and dumping her in a trash bag. He even paused occasionally as if to choke back tears and compose himself before continuing. Naturally, no one had thought to contact him but as soon as he heard ...

"Mr. Jackson, may we then assume it was your child she was carrying?"

"What? She was pregnant? Ohmigod!" A new wave of emotion shook the man's shoulders.

Daniel brought him a glass of water.

"Anything I can do, chief, anything ..."

"Well, I do have a few questions, just routine, of course, now that I know of your involvement."

In short order, Daniel found out that Brian had no idea who Max Vinterra was, had been at his office working that Saturday night, and had checked in with security, they could vouch for him. He spent most of Sunday at the office, too. Then he was at his apartment alone. He had met Garrett Anniston but the man didn't spend much of his valuable time with the junior ADAs.

Finally, after signing a statement Daniel had the clerk quickly type up, he was free. Daniel watched discreetly from a side window as he left. When the man stepped outside the jail, his shoulders straightened and he walked briskly to his car. Well, well, Daniel thought to himself, so it's true what they say: *every good attorney is a good actor.*

Daniel didn't mind admitting that he'd be happy to tie Garrett Anniston to Sally's murder. Bringing down the greedy bastard would be a coup that would resonate for years throughout the entire state. And yes, making him pay for the way he had treated Melissa would be a nice bonus.

Daniel called his cousin, Denise, who worked at the courthouse. Within a minute, she had said that the courthouse had been abuzz when Sally came to visit the new ADA last week. What day was it? Oh, maybe Friday? Yeah, because it was slow and she was thinking TGIF. It was probably after four, because she kept looking at her watch holding out for five. So that seemed to confirm Jackson's story that he and Sally were lovers. That didn't mean he hadn't killed her, though in Daniel's opinion, he was more the type to buy her off than strangle her.

CHAPTER THIRTY-SEVEN

When Jane told her that Mimi wasn't coming down for dinner, Melissa took a tray up to her. Her aunt's narrow face seemed more haggard than it had only yesterday and she simply nodded as Melissa put the food on the bedside table.

Melissa hesitated. "Is there anything I can do for you?" Mimi lowered her eyes and shook her head.

So Melissa went down to dinner with Jane, who chatted cheerfully through the meal and Melissa found herself wondering again if Jane had a man in her life. After helping with the dishes, she thought about calling Stephen but decided to take a long bath instead. She knew she should be working on her book but wound up quietly sitting in bed, mulling over Sally's death, thinking about Daniel.

Half asleep, she began to imagine a warm back lying there beside her and her hand sliding around his waist as he turned over, touching his chest, then his solid thigh. She could hear his breathing change as he enjoyed the slow stroking. He turned slightly towards her and she put her head on his chest. He began touching her in response. His heartbeat quickened. *Oh, Daniel.* She loved the feel of the soft hair on his chest, not too much, just enough. As his body came down on top of hers and she began to move beneath him, she became confused. This body was longer and leaner than she expected. When his hair brushed her cheek, it was straight, smooth hair, Stephen's hair. *Oh, God, Melissa, you are so screwed up.* She shoved the pillow over her head.

She woke up and had trouble catching her breath; she thought at first that it was the pillow choking her. She heard popping and hissing sounds and smelled smoke. She threw herself from the bed. It was dark and she banged into the furniture until she found the door. It wasn't hot. She pushed it open and stumbled down the dark, smoky hallway, calling for Jane.

She tripped over something and fell. She pulled herself back far enough to reach down; she touched soft hair and then a flannel nightgown. *Aunt Jane!* Melissa pulled the limp figure into her arms, rocking back and forth, saying her name. When she didn't respond, Melissa struggled to her feet, trying to hoist the woman up, clutching at the nightgown. She couldn't lift her aunt's heavier body, so she threw an arm around her waist and dragged her down the hall and then down the stairs, wincing as her aunt's feet bounced off each step. *Sirens! Thank God!*

Daniel threw his Jeep into park and was out of it before the engine stopped running. His brother, Tom, was running hoses up the sidewalk to the house. Flames were shooting out of the upstairs windows.

He grabbed Tom's arm. "Anybody come out?"

Tom shook his head and pointed at the emergency rescue squad pulling in further down the street. When he turned, Daniel was already on the steps. Disregarding his training and duty, Tom dropped his hose and followed his brother. Just then the front door opened and Melissa staggered out backwards, dragging Jane by her arms, panting from the smoke and exertion.

Daniel touched her and yelled, "It's all right. I've got her." He picked Jane up and ran toward the ambulance across the street.

Tom took Melissa by the arm and led her toward the ambulance. She knew he was talking to her, but she couldn't seem to understand what he was saying. "MIMI ... IN ... THERE!" she screamed. She shook her arm free and broke back toward the house.

This time, when Tom caught her, he nodded and pointed to himself and shoved her back down the walk. One of the EMTs took her firmly by the arm. Tom raced up the front steps but the fire chief had seen the move and blocked the door, denying him entry. Like everyone else in town, he knew that Mimi was almost totally bedridden these days and that her room was on the second floor.

The chief shook his head sadly. "Can't let you up there, Tom, too dangerous." He laid a gloved hand on Tom's shoulder. "Get back on that hose, boy."

Daniel stayed too, after watching the ambulances pull away. He radioed in all his men and directed them to keep the curious and the concerned at a distance until it was over. When the fire was under control and the crowd of onlookers had gone home, he could justify speeding to the hospital.

When he got to the ICU unit, he spoke to the sad-looking nurse on duty. "Hey, Gloria."

She forced a smile. "Chief. I sure hope you're here for the Sullivan girl."

His face fell. "Where is she?"

"She's still in with Jane." She cleared her throat. "It's been over an hour, honey, and I gotta get her out of there." She sighed. "Gonna have to sedate her, I expect."

"Let me see what I can do."

"I'd appreciate it." She walked down the hall to a door, motioning Daniel to follow.

Through the glass, he could see Melissa sitting next to Jane, holding her hand. The older woman covered with a sheet up to her shoulders.

"Gloria, is Jane, uh ...?" He looked the question at her.

"She died of a heart attack before she hit the floor. We never had a shot. She had a history, you know. Heart problems. And the shock ..."

He pushed the door open. Melissa paid no attention to him. She was talking to her aunt in a soft, childlike voice.

"Come on, Aunt Jane. Wake up. We need to go home now. You know how we hate hospitals, Aunt Jane. We can't be here. Please, wake up."

He gently touched her arm, then crouched down to be on her eye level. "Melissa, it's Daniel."

She turned her head just enough to see him and said, "Hi, Daniel."

"Honey, you have to rest now. You're very tired."

She sighed. "I am tired. But I can't leave." She looked at him reprovingly. "You can see that Aunt Jane is sick, Daniel." She stroked the plump hand.

Daniel glanced at the window and saw Gloria wiping her eyes. He cleared his throat. "Missy, look at me."

Suddenly her face lit up. "I can help her, can't I? I forgot. I can, you know, do the thing." She flexed her hands and raised them over Jane's body.

He grabbed her hands. "No! Missy, you can't. Not now, the nurse is watching."

She looked at Daniel and then the tears overflowed her eyes and ran unchecked down her face. "I can't lose Aunt Jane. I can't. She's the only one who's always loved me, Daniel, you know that." She shook her head stubbornly. Her voice shrank to a tiny whisper. "I can't."

Daniel continued to grasp her cold hands tightly in his own warm ones. "It's gonna be okay, Missy. I promise."

Her chin fell to her chest. After a short silence, she said, "She's dead, isn't she?"

"Yes." He pulled out his handkerchief and wiped her face. She didn't seem to notice.

"I always wind up alone," she said in a forlorn voice.

"You're not alone, Missy."

She laid a cool hand on his tired, dirty face. "You look so tired, Daniel." Then she stood up so abruptly it startled him. "Where's Mimi?"

He stood too and put a firm arm around her shoulders. "Come on. It's time to sleep now. We'll talk tomorrow."

She wiped her eyes with her hands. "She's dead too, isn't she?"

If only he could bring himself to lie to her. He nodded.

She sighed deeply and straightened her back. "So where do you want me to go, Daniel?"

As she was being tucked in and sedated by Gloria and an orderly, she kept her eyes riveted on Daniel. As the shot began to take effect and she was drifting off, she whispered, "Where's Stephen? I need Stephen."

Daniel went home. His mother had been in the living room rocking back and forth rhythmically in her rocker by the window. She rose quickly when she heard the Jeep door slam. She was there when he came through the doorway. One look at his face and she started to cry. The big man folded himself around his mother and they cried together. When she'd gone off to bed, he picked up the phone.

Three in the morning or not, whether it was the last thing in the world he wanted to do or not, there was a call he had to make.

Stephen had finally fallen asleep. When the phone rang, he instinctively reached for it, and then remembered he wasn't on call, "Yes?"

"Callahan, this is Daniel MacBride."

He sat bolt upright in bed and pushed the hair from his eyes. "Is she all right?"

"No, there's been a fire. She's in the hospital."

Stephen inhaled, and then remembered his resolve. "Does she want me to come?"

Daniel was only taken aback for a second. "She's asking for you."

Stephen exhaled. "I'm on my way."

CHAPTER THIRTY-EIGHT

In another house across town, Jill had heard the sirens and turned on the police scanner. *The Witherspoon house!* Oh my God, it must be Sam. If only she could keep him away from Max Vinterra.

The front door shut with a click and he tiptoed into the bedroom. He made a poor attempt at undressing and climbing into bed without waking her. He was trembling so badly the bed shook. She moved involuntarily and he immediately turned and rolled over against her. She swallowed her tears and stretched her arm. Her husband laid his head on her shoulder.

"What have you done?" She asked quietly.

He told her the truth. Max had given him what he said was a smoke bomb that would get Melissa out of the house. Then Sam could grab her and, well, teach her a lesson. He only wanted her to leave town, he swore. Something went wrong, there was lots of smoke but then it looked like the whole second floor of the house caught fire. Nobody came out, so Sam ran away.

He was beginning to think Max had set him up again. There were rumors about Garrett Anniston wanting Melissa gone for some reason and everybody knew Max did his dirty work. It was so confusing. He didn't mean any real harm to anybody, he swore it. He cried on her shoulder. She calmed him until he closed his eyes and began to snore.

It was so incredibly stupid she could scarcely keep from telling him so. She knew that Daniel MacBride would be coming for him and then it would be out of her hands. The good Lord would surely forgive her if she hoped that they sent him to jail for a really long time.

CHAPTER THIRTY-NINE

As soon as it was daylight, Daniel dragged himself over to One Witherspoon Lane and surveyed the blackened second story of the old place. He spoke with the fire marshal who was poking around, then went inside. He slipped into the small office where Mimi did her bookkeeping.

"If ... when ... anything happens, you get this for her from my desk. I can't trust anyone, even my attorney, the whole town would know. But you ... care ... about Melissa, see that she gets the letter ... please."

Several weeks ago, Daniel had been astonished to receive a call at his office from Mimi herself. Everyone in town knew how sick she was. She had spoken the few sentences with great difficulty and then hung up. He found it just where she said it would be, placed it in the inside pocket of his jacket, and calmly walked back outside to his Jeep.

Instead of going to the office, he went home. He went straight up the stairs, calling to his mother that he'd be down in a few minutes. In an equally weary voice, she answered that the coffee was on.

He closed his door and sat down on the bed with a sigh. The old lady must have known he would read it. His hand trembled slightly as he broke the old-fashioned wax seal and read what should have been read only by the one to whom it was addressed.

My dear Melissa,

Jane has been after me for some time to explain myself to you. If you are reading this, I must never have found the courage to do so. Perhaps it was meant to be that way.

I never married, as you know, and there were reasons for that. My father preferred that I run his household. That sounds rather sanitized to me now, and I realize that, after repeating it all these years, I have removed the sting from the truth. I know you are impatient with less than truth, aren't you, my dear? My father abused me, both physically and emotionally, over the years and would not let me go. Humiliation and shame kept me quiet; money kept me here. Enough about that.

When he finally passed, I was almost 40 and had no idea what to do with my life. I had an affair with a married man. I can envision the shock on your face. Oh, yes, warm blood did flow through these veins for a brief period of time. And then, miracle of miracles or horror of horrors, I discovered I was pregnant. And now you must brace yourself for a shock.

My younger sister, Emily, desperately wanted a child but she could not have one. We pulled off an elaborate hoax and my daughter became hers. I do hope you are sitting down. Now you will look in the mirror and see the white streak in your hair that I have and you have but Emily did not. Now you will recognize the tilt to your smile and wonder why you never noticed mine. Not that I have been given over much to smiling these past years. Now you will think about the "gift" and the X in your left palm that I have and you have but Emily did not. And you will know that it is true; you are my daughter.

Your father would have had me get an abortion. I refused. Abortion is murder and a sin. Then, after your "parents" died and you came back to me, (Ah, yes, God has a sense of humor. He has been laughing at me for decades.) He was very concerned that someone would make a connection back to him. He never intended to acknowledge you, I'm afraid, my poor girl, because he is a politician first and not much else. You deserve to know his name, the bastard is—Garrett Anniston. As I write this, he is the county district attorney, intent on working his way up the political ladder. He still believes he can be governor one day. One can hope not but he is willing to buy and threaten his way to the top; I believe he will kill for it if he has to.

After you came back to me, he badgered me to send you away. You will be surprised to hear that I resisted until it was time for you to go to college. I convinced him it would look obvious and unnatural to do so before. I let you think it was my ambition for you and my desire to be rid of you that put you on that plane but, believe me or not, it was hard to see you go. I knew quite well how desperately you wanted to stay, my Melissa, but I also knew you would be safer if you stayed away.

I obviously miscalculated. It seems there is something here you can't or won't live without. All of the trials and tribulations, all of the self-abuse and self-inflicted failures, were your ways of punishing me for making you leave this place and that something behind. In your indignation and youthful self-righteousness, I can hear you saying we should have fought together, taken the bastard down, and moved on with our lives. Perhaps you are right. But have you forgotten what it's like to live in a small town?

I will now indulge in a postmortem bit of motherly advice, which I am sure you will resent, but I believe I've earned the right to be heard. It is too late, Melissa. You cannot go back to the days when your life was simple. You cannot get your *family back and you cannot stay here and have Daniel's children and live happily ever after.*

Even if you and Daniel could find a way to keep you content here, Garrett will not let you. Please, please, marry your doctor if he loves you. Free yourself from this town and the past. Give yourself over to who you are now, give up the person you expected to be. I know it's not easy. Believe me, I know.

It is hard for me to suggest that you leave the Witherspoon legacy untended in this town. But we have perhaps outlived our usefulness. Yes, the town will be better off without us, I believe. Free rather than abandoned.

I have reason to believe that Daniel knows all or most of what I have just explained to you. He is not stupid and he has watched over you almost as long as I have. But Garrett will know that, too. So, if Daniel turns you away, try to remember that love shows its face in many unexpected ways.

Go in peace, my darling daughter.

Aunt Mimi (Mother)

With shaking hands, Daniel put the letter back in its envelope and tucked it between the pages of his Bible. The news about Anniston being Melissa's father wasn't a surprise, since he'd heard it from Sally. He had known it was true—something about the way Anniston ran a hand through his hair, something familiar about the golden-brown eyes.

But with the revelation of an illegitimate daughter, Anniston could kiss his political career good-bye—and his marriage. Cynthia Forester Anniston, the daughter of a former governor, had chosen Garrett to be her ticket back to the governor's mansion, maybe even the White House. She was a power in her own right in the state and there was no doubt that she would lead the pack to crucify him if this ever came out.

This fragile piece of paper was a lit stick of dynamite and should never be seen by anyone but Melissa. If he gave it to her while she was still in Sylvan Mills, there was a damn good chance she'd go straight at Anniston, putting her life in danger. Or was he simply interested in keeping the peace? Did it really matter?

He washed his face and choked down a quick and quiet lunch with his mother before calling the hospital to check on Melissa.

She had some smoke inhalation but was going to be okay. Every muscle in him ached to go to her, but it wasn't his place. And he needed some time to prepare himself to look her in the eye and lie to her.

CHAPTER FORTY

Stephen had driven from Manhattan in a little under five hours, more than enough time to imagine a hundred different ways Melissa could be critically injured. Maybe MacBride had been so brief on the phone to spare him until he arrived. But she was alive. *She was alive.*

He found the room and opened the door without hesitation. Her eyes were closed and he sat down in the chair beside the bed. He looked her over carefully for signs of trauma. She didn't appear to be in pain, there was that.

Melissa opened her eyes. At the sight of Stephen's thin, anxious face, and of him caught in the act of checking her over for injuries, her control weakened.

"Stephen," she rasped. "How did you ... know?"

He touched her face. "MacBride called me last night." Then it hit him. "He said, uh, that you asked for me."

The tears came into her eyes. "I'm ... so glad ... you're here." She swallowed. "All limbs ... intact, don't worry."

He exhaled deeply and his shoulders lost some of the tension they had held all the way from the city. "Thank God, thank God."

She swallowed. "Stephen ..."

"Maybe you shouldn't try to talk."

She raised a hand to his cheek. Then, to his enormous surprise, she said, "I've been ... such a bitch ... to you."

He gave her a careful grin. "Not always."

That gave her a chance to smile and he smiled back, his own eyes bright and moist. He waited like the patient man he was. Then she surprised him again.

"We need ... to talk."

Whatever it was she had to say to him, he would take it like a man. He answered her firmly. "Okay. But let's hold off a bit, until you're better up for it."

She nodded. He continued to hold her hand.

She took a deep breath and the tears rolled down her face again. "Aunt Jane's gone."

He nodded in sympathy. "I'm so sorry, honey."

He gave her a couple of minutes to compose herself while he brought each of them a cup of tea from the cafeteria.

She coughed, her throat raw. "Mimi's ... gone too. But I ... would have ..."

He stroked her arm. "Of course you would have, I always knew that. You're a good person, Melissa, no matter what you try to make yourself believe."

"You're so annoying ... when ..."

"When I'm being a brilliant psychologist, or a needy boyfriend, or just because I know you so well?"

She chuckled, and then choked. "All of ... the above."

"Are you well enough to leave? Do you want to get out of here?" He gave her a lopsided smile. "I know you hate hospitals."

"Absolutely." She said it so quickly that she coughed again and had to take a sip of tea. "Can I?"

"I'll be right back." He returned quickly from the nurse's station. "That cough and sore throat are due to smoke inhalation. It will take a day or two for your lungs to clear completely. But they'd rather not give you anything else at the moment." He grinned. "So I've talked them into signing you out." He said with satisfaction. "I am a doctor, you know."

"Well done. Now don't ... stand there ... hand me ... my clothes." She coughed and took another sip of her tea. "Ah, nuts, I don't have ... any clothes ... do I?"

"Never fear. I wasn't sure what was going on so I packed you a bag from home, uh, the apartment." He stood. "Why don't I run out to the car and get it? Then we'll find a hotel, if that's okay with you, and settle you in for a bit of a rest while I look into things. It's a small town. I should be able to find my way around."

Melissa knew Stephen as well as he thought he knew her. She had seen in his face that he thought she was going to tell him that she wasn't coming back to him, and yet he continued to take care of things. But she couldn't bring herself to initiate that conversation here. She flashed him a smile and nodded.

Stephen was starting toward the elevator when he heard a door open and turned just in time to see a tall, dark-haired, too damned good-looking doctor enter Melissa's room. He resisted the urge to go back and kick him out.

"Melissa! Dear God, are you okay? I just heard you were here. I came right down." Jake's energy and outburst made Melissa realize how tired she was.

"I'm fine, Jake. Really. And it was … sweet of you … to come."

He dropped into the chair Stephen had just vacated and grabbed her hand. "Are you sure? I could check you over." His eyes ran up and down her sheet-covered body.

He had made her chuckle. "Forget it, you're … too eager." She inhaled and coughed. "My house … burned last night."

His face settled into serious. "Oh, my God, I didn't know. Are your aunts okay? Are they here too?"

All she could do was shake her head, tears rolling down her face.

He was stunned into total silence at first. Then he grabbed a tissue from the side table and wiped her face. "Melissa, I am so sorry. What can I do?"

Stephen had hustled out to the car in record time and now pushed open the door and stood there holding Melissa's suitcase.

Right behind him was Daniel to whom it had occurred that Stephen might not have arrived and Melissa might be at the hospital alone.

Melissa looked at the three of them. On another day, in other circumstances, this might have struck her as funny. Brief introductions were made. Jake mumbled something about discretion being the better part of, etc., etc., gave Melissa a quick wink, and beat a hasty retreat. As he left, he shot back at Stephen and Daniel, "Hey, you guys need a referee or anything, I'm your man."

Daniel turned to Stephen. "I wasn't sure you had arrived. I just wanted to make sure everything was under control here."

Stephen met his gaze evenly, feet planted squarely, and said, "Well, I am here and I think I can handle it, chief."

Melissa found herself noting with an author's fascination the way they had squared off, she could almost smell the testosterone in the room, both of them completely forgetting that she, the object of their bristling, was present. "Hello? Remember me?"

They ended their stare down and both looked at her. She moved the sheets aside and swung her legs over the edge of the bed.

"Stephen ... my clothes, please.

"Daniel ... I'll call you ... as soon as I'm settled. I'll be ... ready to leave ... in ten minutes. Stephen ... my discharge papers ... okay?"

She made it through with only two stops for coughing spells. She let Stephen fuss over her all the way to the hotel room. When he thought she was all tucked in, he went out to find cough drops, bottled water and a restaurant for take-out. Melissa called a cab. She had business to take care of before she could rest.

CHAPTER FORTY-ONE

She rang the bell and when Jill opened it, she said a husky whisper, "I want to see him."

Jill tried to shut the door. "Please, Melissa. That's not a good idea. Maybe we should call Daniel."

"Get out of … my way, Jill." She placed a hand on the door and pushed.

"Jill, who is it?" Sam came out of the bedroom in his boxers, still groggy. His eyes met Melissa's over Jill's head. "What do you want?"

"I'm coming in. Jill, get out … of my way." Melissa shoved her way in. "Surprised to see … me, Sam?" She rasped and cleared her throat.

"What the hell do you want?"

Melissa found her voice weakening but shook it off. "I want you … to admit to my face … that you did it … you son of a bitch."

Sam started to sweat. "Get the hell out of my house."

"Tell me." She took a step forward.

Jill started to cry and tried to step between them. "Please don't. Please, Melissa, leave before you get hurt."

Melissa turned on her. "Don't you ever … get tired … of cleaning up … after this pig? Are you really … that stupid?"

Jill's eyes hardened and she said firmly, "You better go now. I'm calling the police."

Melissa smiled. "Yes, by all means … call the police. What do you … think, Sam?" She looked at Jill and then up at him. "Think we should … get the police over here?"

He was starting to panic. "It's okay, Jill. We can handle this."

"Fine. Just tell me to my face … that you burned down … my house … and killed my family."

"They're dead?" He almost squealed the words. "I swear to God, Melissa ..."

She waved a hand towards him threateningly. "Don't you even ... dare. God wants no part of you ... you worthless bastard."

Sam's eyes narrowed. He reached out with his big, meaty hand and grabbed Melissa by the throat. She swung her foot up, the way she'd learned in self-defense class, and kicked him hard. He doubled over for a minute and came back up with a right hook that would have broken her jaw if she hadn't stepped aside. Jill was screaming. Suddenly, a small boy flew across the room and threw his arms around Sam's knees.

"Daddy, please. Daddy, stop!"

They all froze and looked at Kevin, holding onto Sam and crying, in his brown cowboy pajamas. Jill ran over to the little boy just as the door flew open. Daniel stepped in, gun drawn, with Stephen right behind him.

CHAPTER FORTY-TWO

Daniel never could have imagined a day like this one and he hoped to God he'd never have another one. He had helped Jill get Kevin out of the room before hauling Sam away in cuffs, called Jill's mother to come to take care of her and the boy, and sternly rebuked Melissa before handing her over to Callahan.

Sam's attorney showed up in time to keep him from incriminating everyone he'd ever met. After speaking with his attorney, he went for a deal. The cost of admission was his testimony on Max's confession to Sally's murder. He had no idea of the motive. Daniel did but it was Max's call as to whether he wanted to do the time for the whole slimy bunch or cut his own deal. So far, he had decided to tough it out and wasn't talking.

Daniel wasn't happy about it but that was turning out to be a big club. Anniston was still pissed because Max had screwed up both Sally's murder and getting Melissa out of town. The man had no finesse. He was also irritated because he had gotten a phone call from Daniel suggesting delicately that the one ADA who did not play along with Anniston be assigned to Max's prosecution or Daniel might place a call to the state's attorney.

Jackson wasn't exactly bubbling over; he seemed to keep getting in deeper instead of getting out or at least even. He was starting to lose his enthusiasm for politics. And, much to his surprise and chagrin, he actually missed Sally.

There was no joy across town, either.

"You're not ... listening! Sam killed ... my aunts!" Melissa choked it out through a mixture of smoke inhalation and frustration.

Stephen answered in that angry but controlled voice that drove her nuts. "Melissa, even if that's true, you were in no condition to confront him. That's a job for the police."

"Helloooo. This is a ... small town. The police were in ... over their heads. They couldn't even find ... Sally's killer."

"You're rationalizing." The anger flowed over into Stephen's stern tone. "You nearly got yourself killed today." He didn't stop. "Not to mention traumatizing that poor kid."

"Oh, so now ... it's my fault? Do ... you think it was ... the first time ... he'd seen Sam hit ... a woman? I am a victim here ... goddammit!" she screamed.

She started to cry and couldn't stop. Stephen held out for a good sixty seconds before wrapping his arms around her and murmuring comfort into her hair. It felt so good that Melissa settled down against his chest and closed her eyes. He picked her up and sat down in the one chair in the room. There they stayed for over an hour as she slept and Stephen reminded himself that she needed him now. They had a double funeral to arrange.

As she breathed softly against him, warm and quiet, he reminded himself too that they were going to have the talk. He also tried to remember that he was sure he could live without her if he had to. As long as she was happy, right?

When she awoke with a small sigh, she put her arms around his neck and her lips to his. He put his hand on the back of her head and held her there, kissing her with a passion that left her breathless. She finally pulled away and looked up at him in surprise, panting.

To hell with it! If this was it and it was over, he was going to go out in a blaze of glory. He picked her up and carried her to one of the two double beds.

Or maybe not. Because, after apologizing sweetly for losing it earlier, Melissa said it was time for their "talk."

She pulled herself away from him and patted the other side of the bed.

Stephen took a deep breath and gamely plopped down on the bed next to her. "Are you sure you're up to it?" He was still hoping she wasn't.

She grabbed a water bottle from the table and took a drink. "Yeah, I'm good."

He braced himself and his face settled into stiff anticipation.

"Don't stiffen up ... your face like that. Please, Stephen, relax."

He tried and his face settled into a pained grimace.

"Well, that will ... have to do. Here's the thing, Stephen. Do you know ... what you want ... out of life?"

"Huh?" He was astounded.

"No, it's a very ... important question." She asked soberly "What do you really ... want out of life?"

He got up, went over to the briefcase he carried everywhere, and pulled a piece of paper from a pocket. "All right." He cleared his throat dramatically. "Number One: Melissa. That would be you. Number Two: I want to practice more and teach less. Number Three: I want to publish some articles if I can get someone, that would be, uh, you, to help me write something that someone will actually be able to read. Number Four: I want to travel, see the pyramids in Egypt and all that. Number Five: I want season tickets to Carnegie Hall. Number Six: I want to eat at every four-star-and-up restaurant in Manhattan. Number Seven: I want kids, I think, but I'm willing to be flexible on that last one." He looked down at the paper and then back at her cautiously.

Her eyes narrowed. "There's another one, isn't there? Say it."

"Number Eight: I want to have sex in the shower." He colored slightly.

Melissa realized her mouth was hanging open and clamped it shut. "You have all ... this written down? Why didn't you ever ... show me?"

He frowned. "It's a life list. I thought everybody had one. I guess I wasn't sure you were, well, ready, or maybe even interested. I didn't want to scare you off. It's kind of, well, personal. " He flushed. "Do you think it's silly?"

"No, not at all." She stood up, her face sober, and wrapped her arms around his neck. "In fact, I think ... I can help you ... with that last one."

When he came out of the shower with a towel wrapped around his waist, Melissa was lying on the bed wearing the hotel's bathrobe, a tablet balanced across her legs.

He put a warm hand on her knee. "Making your list?"

She flashed him a tired smile. "I guess over the years ... I've never gotten much past Number One ... which was making Mimi miserable."

He kissed her lightly on the forehead, went over to the other bed, and fell asleep immediately. But Melissa, exhausted though she was, was determined not to sleep until she figured out her own life list. Calling herself shallow, superficial, selfish, and a shrew wasn't very productive, either. *What do I want? What do I want? What do I want? Another bestseller? Review in the NYT Book Section? A baby? Not just no, but hell no!*

I want to go home.

She closed her eyes for a short rest. It was a start.

CHAPTER FORTY-THREE

Melissa had insisted on seeing the house again over Stephen's protests so she couldn't admit to second thoughts when they got out of the car.

She walked through each room on the first floor and then stood looking up the stairs, thinking about the last time she had come down them, dragging Jane's body. Stephen took her firmly by the arm and led her outside just to make sure she didn't try to go beyond the yellow tape.

She was quiet and subdued until she went outside and walked around the back of the house. Then she froze.

The firemen had spared nothing in their efforts to save the Witherspoon Victorian from burning to the ground, certainly not the roses. Scrambling in the dark, they had pulled heavy hoses through the yard destroying everything in their paths. The bushes were knocked down and the roses smashed underfoot. Petals were strewn about the soggy path as if the wedding party had come and gone. The scents of burnt wood and wet earth mingled with perfume of dying flowers. Roof tiles and bits of wood lay tossed throughout further insulting the plants that had been Jane Witherspoon's pride and joy. Her girls as she called them tenderly—Louise, Sally, Zeffie—lay defeated in the mud.

A glitter of light from a stained glass window caught Melissa's eye. She looked up at the indomitable monstrosity of a house, still standing, albeit scorched and sullen. Only the roof, attic and second floor had been damaged by the fire. Melissa Witherspoon Sullivan glared at her family home, boasting the address of One Witherspoon Lane in a town they mostly owned, and thought bitterly that she would gladly have seen the whole place go up in flames if it had saved Jane's roses.

She sank to her knees in the mud and sobbed.

Stephen watched as long as he could, and then pulled her to her feet. She said without looking at him, "This is all my fault."

"Melissa ..." He spoke softly.

"Go ahead and say it. I should have never come back." After one more look at the charred house and the ruined roses, she turned away. As she walked past him, she added in a strangled whisper, "Look what I've done."

Back at the hotel, he got her to drink a glass of water which he dosed with one of the pills the hospital had sent home with her, which she had sworn not to take. Only when she was out cold in the bed did he allow himself to break down. Then he washed his face and went to the small café across the street and brought them back the dinner specials and several large coffees.

The smell of food brought her awake. She took a quick shower and rubbed herself down vigorously, downed a cup of coffee, and pronounced herself ready to discuss the matters at hand. Stephen refused to help her until she ate at least half of the meatloaf with mashed potatoes and peas. She actually seemed tickled by his enjoyment of the comfort food, so different from their diet in New York.

Then, following her instructions, he called Tom MacBride. He asked him to go by the house and estimate repairs. At the same time, she was on her cell speaking with the funeral home, answering their questions, asking her own, and putting the arrangements in order. Seeing the pallor on her face when she finished, Stephen coaxed her into watching an old movie on the small TV, curled up against him on the spongy love seat.

When she was sleeping soundly, he picked her up and tucked her in, relieved at the break. Her seesaw mood swings were not only scary, they were exhausting. He fell asleep shortly thereafter himself, his final thoughts of tomorrow, another dreadful day to get through.

CHAPTER FORTY-FOUR

She would go back one more time, no argument. Melissa searched until she found the album of her clippings and the photos that Jane had shown her: a picture of Emily as a college girl, and a few others, including one of Mimi and Jane, looking absurdly young and painfully full of hope and possibility.

When Tom MacBride knocked lightly, she opened the door. She saw in his face that he was remembering the last time she had opened that door for him. He muttered his condolences. "Melissa, I can't tell you how sorry Annie and I are."

The same memory had struck Melissa but she waved both it and his awkward muttering aside. It was best to focus on the business that needed to be done. "Thanks, Tom, we appreciate it." She looked behind her to where Stephen waited by the library door. "Come on in."

They walked into the library, which was remarkably undamaged except for the smell of smoke that permeated the whole house. Melissa waited until they were all seated and asked Tom if he had completed his estimate of the repairs.

He hastily pulled some yellow papers from his pocket, relief evident on his face at being back on familiar ground. "Okay, you know the place wasn't in the best of shape to begin with, so there's a lot of electrical and heating just to bring it up to code in the first place, even without the fire damage. Here's the written estimate but I can walk you through it if you want."

She smiled but shook her head and refused the paper. "I trust your judgment. Bottom line?"

He looked to Stephen for support. "About eighty to

ninety thousand just to bring her up to code. I, uh, don't know what your insurance is gonna pay. But, if it's done right, given the location and all, the house might be worth about three or four times that, I reckon." He gave her a wry grin. "That's probably small potatoes to New Yorkers, but that's real money around here."

She nodded. "Stephen got a similar figure from a realtor over the phone."

He didn't try to hide his surprise. "You're selling it?"

She reached over to lay a smooth, slim hand over his large, callused one. "No, Tom. I just wanted to make sure I wasn't sticking you with a white elephant."

"What?" He swallowed hard. "I'm sorry but we can't afford ..."

She stopped him. "Hear me out, please. I want this house to have a family. You and Annie need more room. I will sign the house over to you, free and clear. Mimi's attorney is handling everything for me. I've already spoken with him. If you're willing to take it on, all you have to do is call him." She paused. "I know you'll want to talk it over with Annie, but nothing would make me happier."

Tom's eyes had grown large. "I don't know what to say." Then his face fell. "I guess this means you're not staying, are you?"

Melissa looked at Stephen, who moved to put his arm around her shoulder. "I don't think so. After the funeral, I'm going home."

CHAPTER FORTY-FIVE

Most of the county seemed to turn out for the funerals of Melissa and Jane Witherspoon. Stephen was thinking that although he had projected so many possible complications in Melissa's return home, none of them touched on anything close to this day. He was seeing a vulnerable side of Melissa he had never imagined. She was leaning on him, both physically and emotionally. He was happy about that but wished that the cost had not been so dear.

Thanks to the prescription sedative Stephen had slipped into her coffee, the day was a gentle blur for Melissa. It was as if she was attending the funerals of someone else's family. There were only two times that she was aware of all the people around her.

The first time, sobbing from the pew behind her caused her to turn to see a large, balding man with red cheeks and a white handkerchief pressed to his eyes. When she saw the raw pain in his face, Melissa knew she had discovered Jane's gentleman caller and instinctively stretched her hand out toward him.

He grasped her fingers tightly. "I loved her so much," he whispered hoarsely. "We were gonna get married after ..." She stood and leaned toward him and he pulled her into a gentle hug. "I'm so sorry," she whispered, her eyes wet. "I loved her too."

Over his shoulder, in the back row, a tall and distinguished-looking man with thick white hair caught her attention. Their eyes locked for only a second. Melissa had the oddest feeling that she knew him. As she left the church, she looked for him but the place where he had been standing was now empty.

She remained composed until they started shoveling dirt

onto the two side-by-side caskets. Then, if not for Stephen's arm around her waist, she would have fallen forward into the grave.

Because of the fire damage to the Witherspoon house, there was no gathering after the graveside ceremony. For that, Stephen was grateful, even though it would have been unconscionable to say so. As they made their way to the cars, all the characters of Melissa's childhood he would have been delighted to meet under any other circumstances introduced themselves as they went past him, barely registering as he kept an arm around Melissa.

One woman, tears drying on her cheeks, grasped both of Melissa's hands without speaking. Melissa met her eyes and said softly, "Mrs. Hayden?" which cause a fresh flood of tears. Stephen assumed the woman was an old friend of Jane's. In fact, she had been.

At one point, two well-dressed young women came up.

"Oh my God. Madison. Magee. I didn't know ... I didn't expect ..." Melissa struggled to speak clearly.

The taller one, with long dark hair plaited into a braid hanging over her shoulder and deep brown eyes, put out her hand to Stephen. "I'm Madison. We spoke on the phone. I never dreamed we'd meet like this." She paused. "And this is Magee. We're both delighted to finally meet you but wish it weren't under such terrible circumstances."

"I'm so glad to meet you both and thanks for coming. I'm sure it means a lot to Melissa." He leaned toward her and lowered his voice. "She's still suffering from the smoke inhalation and shock I'm afraid. I had to give her a sedative this morning to help her get through the day."

After shaking Stephen's hand, Magee took both of Melissa's hands in hers and closed her eyes for a brief minute. It was just a split second and would have gone unnoticed by anyone watching. But Stephen had seen the brief flash of pain that crossed her face just before she let go of Melissa's hands and stepped back. Stephen suspected he had just seen something special but he couldn't be sure. Magee ran her hand through her long red curls and took a deep breath. Stephen thanked them for coming and promised Melissa would be in touch. As soon as he possibly could, he took her back to the hotel for some peace and quiet.

But Melissa, suddenly focused, took one look around the room and declared, "No, I cannot sit here and feel bad. We have things to do." She turned to Stephen with a stern look. "Are you going to help me or not?" He knew the right answer: "Yes, dear."

So they negotiated, Melissa ate a few bites of a sandwich that Stephen kept putting in front of her while she made a list of people to call and he followed her instructions. Within a minute, they were each on their cell phones.

"I want to speak with you—alone."

Daniel answered slowly. "I don't know about you, Melissa, but I'm about done in for today."

Melissa caught her breath as a thought came to her, "Daniel, where is Sally?"

He became brusque, which told her that talking about it hurt. "Jackson offered to pay for everything but Johnny only wanted to have her cremated and interred at the cemetery with no service. He said he wasn't about to give this town another shot at making fun of her." He cleared his throat. "I've got some social services folks trying to get Johnny into Willow Creek Rehab so he won't die out there alone." He took a breath. "How does two o'clock tomorrow sound? And where?"

She had already figured out this part. "Your house, if that's okay."

"Fine. I'll pick you up at the hotel."

CHAPTER FORTY-SIX

The next afternoon she stood looking out the window at the breathtaking view before she took a deep breath and turned to face him. "I believe I know some things that you don't, Daniel, and I'm fairly confident that you know some things you haven't shared with me."

Before he could open his mouth, she continued. "First, I don't think for a minute that Max just killed Sally accidentally and then panicked and threw her body in the dump," she turned to face him, "and neither do you."

His face stiffened. "Melissa, Max confessed. He killed Sally. I believe that. Motive isn't a critical element in putting him away. Leave it alone."

A thoughtful expression crossed her face. "Okay." She sighed. "Moving on, Jane asked me to help Mimi, at the end, you know, with the pain."

His eyebrows went up.

"Yeah. It was ... hard but I did try. And then she wouldn't let me. After that Jane told me that Mimi was my real mother. She gave me to her sister to raise and then it was, I guess, rotten luck that I came back to her after my, uh, parents' accident. That makes me a little less angry with her, I guess. It must have really rattled her to have me living with her. She liked to deal with problems head-on and then be done with them." She gave him a brief smile. "I would have helped her and knowing that makes it a little easier for me." She paused.

"Jane wouldn't tell me who my real father is, though. She said that was up to Mimi. But, frankly, if he doesn't care about me, I don't care about him. I've gotten along without him all these years.

"The last thing is that you're right, I'm leaving again.

There has always been a part of me that wanted to come home, but it's taken me a while to figure out where my home is. Well, it's not One Witherspoon Lane. It's not Sylvan Mills, not anymore. I think what I really wanted was to go back in time to when I was a kid and have my parents back and have my life take the course it might have taken had they still been alive. Biological or not, no parents ever made a kid feel more special than Rob and Emily Sullivan made me feel."

She sighed. "But I'm a grownup now. I have to start taking responsibility for myself and stop blaming Mimi for everything. My therapist will be totally impressed. That's all I wanted to say." She let out her breath in relief.

Daniel swallowed the lump in his throat and took the woman he loved in his arms. He spoke quietly into her ear.

"It's not fair that we didn't have our chance, Melissa."

He looked into her filling eyes then stepped back and placed his hands on her shoulders. "But it never would have worked out. I'm an ordinary kind of guy. I like to hunt and fish. I read maybe one book a year. I've never seen a Broadway show or been to a ballet. And you know what? That's fine with me." He responded to the look in her eyes. "That's right, and it's fine with Jennifer. You bring out the worst in her because she's so threatened by you, and I think we both understand that. It's because you and I were never really over till now.

"Let me tell you a little bit about Jennifer." He smiled at her expression. "But not too much. When we were in high school, her dad was one of those quiet drunks who took it out on his wife and kid. She hid a lot of bruises under that heavy makeup everyone made fun of. When he fell down the concrete stairs outside George's Tavern and broke his neck, she and her mother breathed freely for the first time in years. She loves kids and wants a chance to have her own. To keep them clean, safe, and loved in a way she never was."

"She fits you," she whispered.

"If I let her," Daniel responded softly. "What about Stephen? Does he fit you?"

Melissa managed a rueful grin. "He might. We're working on it." Then she added, "But you'll always be ..."

"... my first love," he finished for her.

She held onto her smile. "And I'll always wonder ..."

"... what our lives might have been like."

"Now there's one last thing I'd like to do before I leave." Melissa said with a smile.

Daniel looked concerned.

"Don't be afraid. I'm not after your body. Well, not all of it. I'm not sure I have the strength to fight Jennifer today. Please just close your eyes and trust me." She reached up and put her hands on both sides of his neck. He stood very still resisting the urge to stop her but just too curious to try.

She closed her eyes and stepped back after a minute or so, rotating her neck. "Whoa, that really hurts."

When the warmth that flooded through him subsided, Daniel automatically tried to crack his neck as he'd always done to relieve the old football injury that had never healed properly. But his head moved fluidly from side to side. He broke out into a grin.

"Thanks."

"You're welcome."

A car door slammed outside. Seconds later Jennifer stormed in. "I knew it! I knew I'd find you here with her!" She took a deep breath to sustain the next rant but Melissa stepped forward.

"I was just saying goodbye." She said softly.

Jennifer stopped and looked at Melissa's tired, sad face, and burst into tears. Melissa put her arms around the smaller woman and then glanced down at her stomach and back to Jennifer's face. Jennifer's eyes widened but she shook her head. Melissa turned to go.

"Jennifer, be happy. I hope it's a lovely wedding." Then, on a mischievous impulse, she added. "Can I come?"

Without hesitation, Jennifer answered. "Hell, no!"

Melissa chuckled. "Good answer. Daniel, I'll take the jeep and you can pick it up at the hotel."

CHAPTER FORTY-SEVEN

She turned around in her seat and took a final look at the town as they started climbing through the mountains. It was the end of an era; the end of Sylvan Mills as she and many others had known it. The Witherspoons would no longer *be* Sylvan Mills. She knew that there would be a wave of melancholy, a sense of loss that would hit her now and then. *Fair enough.*

"Ten days."

He looked over at her.

"I was there for only ten days." She said softly.

"Seemed longer." They said in unison and they both laughed.

After an hour on the road had passed in silence as she and Stephen both absorbed the tumultuous events of the past few days, Melissa looked over at him. She noticed that he was careful not to tailgate, looked in his rearview constantly, and had both hands correctly position on the wheel while maintaining a constant speed (even if it was the supposedly permissible nine miles over the limit). A smile creased her face. That was her Stephen, following the rules but sometimes ... with a little room for interpretation. Stephen felt her eyes on him and removed one hand from the wheel to squeeze her hand.

"I love you, Stephen." She said it and meant it. "You are going to ask me to marry you, aren't you?"

Stephen jerked the wheel hard to the right and pulled off the highway. He turned to face her, his eyes misty, and said slowly in a precise voice, "I love you too. And yes, I am." With a mischievous grin, he cleared his throat and pulled cautiously back into traffic.

Melissa said, "Ahhh..." in surprise and then started to

laugh uncontrollably which soon turned into crying uncontrollably. She cried for at least a half hour and then just as suddenly stopped. During that entire time, Stephen didn't say a word. He was good that way. Finally, she blew her nose, wiped her eyes, and opened her laptop.

She proceeded to type an email to her cousins inviting them to her wedding, date to be determined. It was wonderful to know that they were her family and would continue to be involved in her life. She assured them that it would be a big party if the Callahans had any say in it.

Daniel knew when she was gone. Young Pete at the gas station had told everyone he knew that she was letting him drive her precious Mustang all the way to New York and then he was coming back on the train! But Daniel would have known even if the grapevine wasn't burning up with the news. It was as if the entire town breathed a collective sigh of relief.

He was learning to live with guilt or at least guilty knowledge. It was enough for now knowing that Melissa was going to be all right. She knew enough to move on with her life. The old man wanted her gone and she was gone. Daniel had made compromises to hold onto his relatively normal life.

But, one of these days, maybe after the old man was dead, or maybe when he had become half as tough as Melissa Witherspoon Sullivan, he would mail her mother's letter.

Epilogue

Stephen fidgeted with his napkin and looked at his watch. He called the waiter over and ordered a bottle of house red to go with his breadsticks.

Tiffany barreled in and slid into her chair, clearly breathless. "Sorry. I had to work late and had a bitch of a time getting a taxi."

He nodded acceptance and handed her the menu. Once their orders were safely placed, he looked at her face carefully. "So what's up?" He asked gently.

She reached up and pulled a pin out of her chignon and her blond hair cascaded down her back as she gave her head a shake. Her blue eyes were filling as she struggled not to cry. "Francois and me, it's ... so hard."

"Tell me about it."

Tiffany outlined the problems with her almost perfect French chef fiancé. He worked so many nights, she worked days. He worked weekends. Could you even believe he didn't like to cook at home?

When she seemed to have reached a stopping point in her rant, Stephen placed his hand over hers on the table. "Tiff, do you want my advice or do you just want to be heard?"

The psychologist-speak made her smile for the first time. "I think I want advice, but I'll let you know after I've heard it." She said in typical Tiffany style.

"Well, here's the thing and you know I have your best interests at heart. You are a wee bit rigid, Tiff."

She stiffened as he had known she would.

"Hear me out now. You sabotage your relationships by expecting the guy to do all the changing—to form his life around yours. You have to show some give, some commitment to making this work. Let me give you a heads up. You are in charge of your department, right? You have a great assistant who does not want your job, right? And your deadlines are more a day thing than an hourly thing, like the publishing department needs your graphics on Monday rather than by two o'clock today, right?" She nodded.

"Right."

He took a breath. "So why don't you change your hours? He can't, you know, people eat when they eat. But you can easily have your assistant hold the fort until noon or whenever so you can have the morning with Francois. And you can do a bunch of work on Saturday or Sunday since he's working then and take off a Monday or Tuesday when he's off. He'll see that you really want this to work. Problem solved. Everything else is negotiable."

"Ohmigod." Tiffany breathed and her face lit up. "You're brilliant. And I forgive you for that rigid and sabotage crap."

They enjoyed the rest of their dinner and Stephen made her laugh with carefully anonymous and annotated tales of his patients and their issues, so much more complicated than hers.

Finally, as he was paying the check, she asked, "How is Melissa?"

Stephen smiled. "Good, she's good."

Tiffany leaned toward him. "I know all the stuff about her aunts and everything was horrible beyond words. But I guess what I want to say is, this ... getting over your first love thing that sort of started all this, what she's been going through ... it's not easy, you know." Her eyes glistened in the table candlelight.

Stephen pushed his chair back, picked up her wrap from the back of her chair and brought it up around her shoulders, letting his warm hands rest there for a few moments, and said, "I know, Tiff, I know."

And yet there's more ...
One Year Later

Dear Reader, for those of you who just have to know the rest of the story, here goes ...

IN SYLVAN MILLS

DANIEL MACBRIDE
Daniel and Jennifer married in September and in January became the parents of a beautiful baby girl, whom they named Ellen Louise after her grandmothers. They are now trying for a boy.

JILLIAN GRAY
Jillian divorced Sam after he was sentenced to a long stretch in prison. She and Kevin are both receiving counseling and Jillian is helping out at a local women's shelter. She sold her house and is living in a new condo complex near the edge of town.

DR. JAKE CAPELLI
Having finished his residency and satisfied his father, Jake has moved to San Diego where, as a single attractive doctor, he is very popular, despite his specialty.

DONNA O'NEIL
Donna was thrilled to be asked to join the Board of Directors of the Witherspoon Memorial Fund, a non-profit Melissa established to control the Witherspoon assets. She married Howard in May. They have no children but three cats and two dogs.

ANNETTE HAYDEN

Much to her surprise, Melissa asked Annette to serve on the Board of the Witherspoon Memorial Fund. Annette and Ellen MacBride are planning a weekend trip to New York to see a Broadway play and will be staying with Stephen and Melissa.

TOM AND ANNIE MACBRIDE

Tom and Annie MacBride have been blessed with a second child, a baby girl. Melissa sent a baptism gift, a ceramic piggy bank with a red rose and the baby's name, *JANE*, painted on the side.

GARRETT ANNISTON

Garrett Anniston was running for the office of Attorney General when he was felled by a stroke. He passed away, leaving everything to his wife, who owned most of it anyway, but designated a bequest to Melissa which she turned over to the Witherspoon Memorial Fund.

BRIAN JACKSON

Brian Jackson resigned his position and went home. He lives with his parents and went back to college and is re-thinking his career options.

PETE MORAN

And Pete, the boy who worked at the gas station, returned Melissa's car safely to New York, and is now in training to become one of Daniel's deputies.

IN NEW YORK

STEPHEN CALLAHAN
Stephen waited weeks to formally propose until it could be completely unexpected and did it on the roof of the Stratosphere Hotel in Las Vegas. Melissa and Stephen tied the knot in a Vegas wedding chapel, much to his parents' initial dismay.

However, the Callahans immediately began planning a big party for the happy couple and included Melissa's cousins in the festivities.

When they returned, Melissa found that their spare room had been partially converted to a solarium filled with transplanted roses from Jane's garden. It was her wedding present from Stephen.

MELISSA WITHERSPOON SULLIVAN
Melissa finished writing her second book about a young woman full of dreams but without a chance in a small town riddled with secrets and corruption. The book was dedicated to Sally. After she received Mimi's letter from Daniel, she sent him a copy of her new book but destroyed the diary. She and Stephen have added a temperamental Yorkie named Bentley to their family.

And incidentally, while she gave the Witherspoon Memorial Fund most of the real estate and corporate assets, Melissa did keep the $1 million plus that Mimi had in her bank account when she died.

She hasn't had time to work on that life list but she has achieved the one item on it so far: *Melissa is finally home.*

Meet the authors...

Mary Devlin Lynch and Debbie Devlin Zook are sisters who have been avid readers since childhood. They discovered a few years ago that they also share a passion for writing. BURNT ROSES is their second Witherspoon novel.

Beth Devlin-Keune
"My life has revolved around sports—and animals. I graduated from Penn State where I was a member of the softball team and somehow usually find myself coaching. My partner of 25 years and I have lots of cats and an incredible mini-dachsund named Renee O'Connor. I own a pool cleaning service, renovate houses, read voraciously, and enjoyed coming to the writing table with my sisters on BURNT ROSES, hopefully more to come."

Other Books
by Mary Devlin Lynch and Debbie Devlin Zook

The Witherspoon Adventures:
Beautiful Disaster (Magee)
Before Everafter (Madison)

The Cayden Wright Adventure Series:
The Wright Move
The Wright One
The Wright Woman

Lying for a Living: Meredith Abbott's
Adventures in Hollywood

We invite you to let us know what you think about any of our books any time. We appreciate reviews on Amazon or Barnes & Noble. Please feel free to email us or post comments on our blog. You are our audience and any feedback you give us will only make our next book better!

E-mail: devlinsbooks@gmail.com
Facebook: devlinsbooks
Twitter: @devlinsbooks
Blog: www.devlinsbooks.com

,